TO AO

KJK PRESENTS
WEREWOLVES

TIM CURRAN GRAHAM MASTERTON KEVIN J. KENNEDY
GRAEME REYNOLDS EDWARD LEE TOM DEADY
CANDACE NOLA GLENN ROLFE

FROM KSV

Werewolves

KJK Publishing

Werewolves © 2024 Kevin J. Kennedy

Edited by Ann Keeran & Kevin J. Kennedy

Cover design by Michael Bray

All rights reserved. No part of this publication may be reproduced, distributed, or transmitted in any form or by any means, including photocopying, recording, or other electronic or mechanical methods, without the prior written permission of the publisher, except in the case of brief quotations embodied in critical reviews and certain other non-commercial uses permitted by copyright law.

First Printing, 2024

Other Books by KJK Publishing

Collections
Dark Thoughts
Vampiro and Other Strange Tales of the Macabre
Merry Fuckin' Christmas and Other Yuletide Shit!
The A to Z of Horror

Anthologies
Collected Christmas Horror Shorts
Collected Easter Horror Shorts
Collected Halloween Horror Shorts
Collected Christmas Horror Shorts 2
Collected Christmas Horror Shorts 3
The Horror Collection: Gold Edition
The Horror Collection: Black Edition
The Horror Collection: Purple Edition
The Horror Collection: White Edition
The Horror Collection: Silver Edition
The Horror Collection: Pink Edition
The Horror Collection: Emerald Edition
The Horror Collection: Pumpkin Edition
The Horror Collection: Yellow Edition
The Horror Collection: Ruby Edition
The Horror Collection: Extreme Edition
The Horror Collection: Nightmare Edition
The Horror Collection: Sapphire Edition
The Horror Collection: The Lost Edition
The Horror Collection: LGBTQIA+ Edition
The Horror Collection: Monster Edition
The Horror Collection: Sci-Fi Edition
The Horror Collection: Turquoise Edition

100 Word Horrors
100 Word Horrors 2
100 Word Horrors 3
100 Word Horrors 4
Carnival of Horror
Inside the Indie Horror World (Non fiction)
Vampires

Novels and Novellas
Pandemonium by J.C. Michael
You Only Get One Shot by Kevin J. Kennedy & J.C. Michael
Screechers by Kevin J. Kennedy & Christina Bergling
Stitches by Steven Stacy & Kevin J. Kennedy
Halloween Land by Kevin J. Kennedy

Dedication

I'd like to dedicate this book to everyone that works with me, and everyone who continues to support KJK Publishing. Working in the horror industry has been a bit of a dream. I am an avid reader and now I get to approach my favourite authors, ask them to write a story for me in a theme that I want to read, get to see the story before almost anyone else and package it with other stories that I've enjoyed. Putting a book together is a lot of work, but it is a lot of fun too. I have worked with some amazing talent over the years, and I consider myself very lucky. None of this would be possible without the amazing horror crowd that continues to buy my books. From myself, my Editor Ann, and all of the fantastic authors that work with KJK Publishing, we thank you from the bottom of our hearts. You allow us to live our passion.

Kev

Elena

Kevin J. Kennedy

Last Dance

Tom Deady

Inherent

Candace Nola

Beware the Moon

Graeme Reynolds

Rug

Graham Masterton

"Harry's Inevitable Extinction"

Glenn Rolfe

Wetware

Tim Curran

Almost Never

By Edward Lee

Elena
By
Kevin J. Kennedy

Touring the Highlands had always been a dream of Elena and Martin. They had rented a cheap camper van that they weren't entirely sure would make the journey and filled it with some clothes, some food, some booze 'n' some weed and set off.

The first days of the journey had begun by stopping at quaint little farm stores, antiques warehouses, and all the small local family run bakeries that they had been so eager to try. These were all in little surrounding towns but after a few days of it, they decided they would head out into the hills where there was practically nothing and find some scenic places to park up and spend the night.

They had plenty to munch on and restocked the booze with a crate of Tennents, a few bottles of Buckfast and a bottle of Aberlour A'bunadh. Plenty to keep them going for a few days. They looked at some maps online and picked a place that looked completely deserted, away from everyone else. Something they never experienced, having always lived in the city.

The journey was beautiful. Sprawling green hills, farms with horses, sheep, pigs, cows and all manner of animals. As they went further on, the farms stopped and the animals they saw after that were wild. They made jokes about the animals having once lived in farms but had made daring escapes to live a free life. As the sun began dipping, they decided to pull into a field at the bottom of a massive hill. They parked up, grabbed a few cans of beer and sat together, holding hands and watching the sun go down out of the large back window of the campervan.

"This is perfect." Elena said.

"It really is." Martin agreed, looking her over before leaning in and kissing her cheek. "I love you."

She loved him too. They had been together ten years and sometimes it felt like a year. They had both had previous long-term relationships, but this was the first for each that had been truly enjoyable.

They set up their mini-DVD player on the main table and picked The Hills Have Eyes. The original version. They drank a few cans each then opened a bottle of Buckfast and passed it back and forward between them.

As soon as the movie finished, Elena said, "Let's fuck!"

She had her top off before Martin knew it, unclipped her bra and threw it across the camper, leaned in next to Martin and unzipped his jeans as she ducked her head down. Her mouth engulfed him. She had always been good at deep throating, having practiced on a banana for a while in order to try and win over the guy she had fancied when she was sixteen. She had heard he had a big dick and had wanted to impress him. When she finally sucked his dick, it had shot its muck down her throat after three or four bobs of the head. He had never spoken to her again. She never really wanted to see him after that.

"Woah there lady. Come up for air. You'll have my nuts empty before I get in your guts," he said laughing.

Elena had always loved when Martin spoke dirty to her.

"Get up here and get your ass bent over this table."

As Elena came up, she slid her jeans and panties down in one swoop. She stepped out of them, put a leg at either side of Martin's and bent over the table. Martin put his tongue straight in her ass. There was no point with starting with her pussy. She was already dripping, and it was her ass he was going to fuck. She always came harder that way, and when he was drinking, he preferred the extra tightness to suck the juice from his balls. Elena moaned as he got his tongue in deep. He moaned into her ass knowing it turned her on before he slid three fingers into her meat cave. She started cumming on his fingers straight away. He then leant over her and stuffed those fingers in her mouth. She sucked them furiously. As she sucked, he lined his dick up and slipped up her shitter. She moaned around his fingers. He fucked her hard and fast, leaning on her lower back, holding her on the table as he went deep. She moaned, 'daddy' as he fucked her. When he was ready to burst, he pulled out and shot his nut from her ass to her hair. He was heavy breathing, and she was still moaning as she teased the last orgasm from her clit with her fingers.

Just as they both finished, the whole inside of the camper lit up with a light coming from outside.

"What the fuck?" Martin said.

Different coloured lights danced all around the camper. They seemed to be coming in from the front window. Dick swinging, still engorged, Martin made his way to the front of the camper. Inexplicably, there seemed to be a pub a little further up the hill. It looked like an old school tavern. The lights were coming from a load of neon signs. Not only did you never see neon signs in Scotland, but Martin was sure there was no pub on the hill when they parked. Could he have missed it because the lights weren't on? Maybe the mist on the hills had hidden it.

"Fancy another few drinks, baby?"

Elena, now with her jeans and panties pulled up but shirt still open and her tits swaying, smiled.

"What else were we going to do? You are going to need a little while for those nuts to fill up again." She grabbed his nuts and pushed her tits into his chest. He started to grow again.

"Not yet. Let's go get a few pints from a tap before we get back to it. And maybe move the camper, unless you wana give them a show. She grinned as she turned to get dressed.

***

Martin wore jeans and a tight woollen top that hugged his muscles and Elena had opted for a little, tight, short black dress. They both had boots on because it had rained earlier and the ground was muddy. When they opened the door, they had expected it to be a few locals and thought everyone would turn and look at them. They were both surprised to see the place was jumping. Rock music played from an old juke box. There were a few bar staff on to keep up with the demand. Some people danced and others sat at tables.

"Where the fuck did all these people come from?" Martin asked.

"Who cares, baby. Let's get a fucking drink."

They made their way to the bar and a short redhead came over and took their order. Two pints and two shots. They knocked back the shots, took a good drink of their beer and looked around the crowd. No one seemed to be bothering with them.

"They must get strangers coming in pretty often." Elena said, wondering why no one was paying her any notice. She spread her legs a little further on the bar stool. She had opted for no panties. She was not used to getting no attention 'n' hoped this might help her catch a few eyes. Not that she would cheat on Martin but if the right girl caught her eye, they might both take her home and fuck her. It had been a while since she had last eaten a pussy and Martin was due for a treat.

'I'm a Maniac' by Zander Gribben's Woolly Panthers came on the juke box and the place got rowdier. The couple drank pint after pint and had a shot with each one. Coupled with the drink they had consumed earlier, they were both pretty wasted.

"Want to go back to the van and do a few lines then I'll blow the hole off you?"

Martin grinned when he said it. He knew she hated that phrase but it just made him use it more. The other one was after sex when he would describe it as 'he had been hanging out of her.' She laughed and punched him on the arm. Just as they were about to go, the redhead approached them.

"Going so soon? I just got off shift" she said.

Elena smiled at Martin in a *We should fuck her* kind of way.

"Suppose we could stay for another few. We have some drink back in the camper though if you would prefer somewhere more private?" Elena said.

"Even better. Let me grab my bag."

They watched her walk away. She was small and slim, and her hair covered her ass which was probably good because her skirt barely did.

All three left together and made the short walk back to the camper. Elena entered first and Martin helped the barmaid in by slipping his hand up her skirt and cupping her ass as she stepped up the stairs. She never commented.

"I'm Isla by the way. Probably shoulda said"

"Martin and Elena," Elena said.

"So, Isla. We were going to do a few lines. Would you care for a line, or would you prefer a drink? Also, help yourself to the weed on the table," Martin said.

"How about a line, a drink and I'll build a joint?"
"Sounds fair."

Martin poured three large glasses of Aberlour neat, grabbed a little mirror they had brought, poured out some coke and chopped it into three lines. He returned to the table where the two girls were sitting on one side facing him and sat the mirror down and gave them a drink each. He returned to the kitchen area and grabbed three beers. Isla had built the joint already and was smoking it. She passed it over to Elena. Picked up the cut off piece of straw and sniffed her line before passing the straw to Martin. Martin did a line quickly and passed to Elena. They sat for around three minutes before Isla asked, "So, you guys did bring me back here to fuck, right?"

They smiled at each other. "Of course," Elena said. "Why else."

And with that the girls were kissing each other ravenously. Martin put out a few more lines, sniffed one and downed his malt. Elena tore Isla's top off. She wore no bra and each of their hands went between the other legs. Martin stripped off completely and lit the joint while he watched. He started to stroke his cock that was already hard. Isla got up, slid her skirt down her legs to show that she too wasn't wearing panties. She lifted the mirror and placed it on the chair. She then slid everything else on the table to the side and lay back on it.

"How about, you go on my face Elena and Martin can fuck me?" Isla asked.

Elena loved riding other girls faces and hadn't done it for so long. She didn't even step out of her dress. She rolled it up to her waste and climbed onto Isla's face, feeling her tongue enter her instantly. She pulled the top of the dress down so Martin could see her tits. He was stood watching them. He finished his joint and flicked it in the sink. Everything was still lit by the neon signs from the bar throwing different colours over everything. In the booze filled, drugged up state it added a heightened element of eroticism. Elena began to moan, and Martin walked over, spat in his hand and rubbed it into Isla's already soaking pussy. He could hear her moaning into Elena's pussy as Elena's moans also began to grow. He slammed his dick home and began to ride her as he watched Elena writhe on her face. Elena's moaning grew in intensity. Martin knew she was about to come and then he would pile them on top of each other and move between all of their holes.

That was when Elena screamed.

Not a normal scream that you would expect from a woman orgasming, not even Elena. The type of scream someone makes when they are being murdered or tortured. Martin pulled out. He stepped back in shock. Elena's face was a picture of exquisite pain. Her eyes closed and her hands held out towards him as if begging for help.

Not knowing what exactly was going on, Martin flipped the camper van lights on. The gorgeous girls face that Elena had been sitting on had sprouted fur. It was still growing, and it was everywhere. The two previously stunning legs that Martin had just been between were hairier than any mans legs he had ever seen. His mind whirled and that's when he sa the blood. It was covering Elena's thighs. They were scarlet and the beast below her had its hands clamped around her holding her in place. It had a snout now and it was actually eating her pussy. Not in a pleasurable way. Biting chunks out of it the way a dog attacks a bone. Martin ran to the kitchen and pulled the drawers open. No big knives. They hadn't brought any. The only thing Martin could grab was the Whisky bottle. As he ran back to them, the first thing that caught his eyes was an extremely large penis seemed to be growing out of what was Isla's pussy. It was enormous, larger than his own. As he got closer the beast threw Elena and she went straight through the side window.

    Martin dove at the beast and smashed the bottle over its head and then plunged a shard of glass that remained in his hand, straight into its throat. Blood splattered everywhere for the large spray that erupted. Martin looked for anything else to hit it with but there was nothing. The beast threw him on the couch and walked over. It lifted the mirror and licked up the rest of the coke from the mirror. The blood had stopped spraying from its neck already and it seemed to be absolutely fine. It grabbed Martin and lifted him in the air, turned him around and bent him over the table. In one thrust, it shoved enough cock inside him to rupture something. He felt it. He didn't know what had broke but he knew he wasn't the same. The creature thrust into him as it tore chunks from his back. Just as it was about to explode, it ripped his head from his shoulders and finished by fucking his neck stump. Once its balls were empty, it slowly began to turn back into the beautiful site of Isla. All woman, all naked and completely bathed in blood. She sat down and built another joint. She lit it and threw Martin's head out of the window. As she did a hand came over the edge. It was Elena. She pulled herself back inside and sat next to Isla. Her pussy was back, and looked better than it ever had. She felt like her hymen had grown back.

"You're one of us now baby. You start in the bar tomorrow night at sundown. Get rid of this camper first and make sure no one finds it." Isla said.

Elena smiled and leant in to kiss Isla. Both were covered in blood. They kissed for a while, eyes glinting yellow and catlike as the moon caught them.

"What about Martin?" Elena asked.

"He won't come back, baby girl. We didn't need any more boys. In fact. Once you know what you are doing, maybe me and you will talk about making this an all-girls place.

The two of them spent the rest of the night fucking and biting chunks from each other that quickly grew back. Elena almost orgasmed every time the blood squirted down her throat. She was going to enjoy this new life. Martin had been a great fuck but Isla was going to show her a whole new world

The End

Last Dance
By
Tom Deady

I shuffle downstairs to the kitchen and plop myself down at the table. My parents look up from their breakfast, exchange a look, then Mom goes to fetch me a plate.

"You want two eggs or three?" Mom asks.

"Three," I say. "I'm starving."

Dad studies me, sneaking a glance at Mom, then says, "Everything all right, son? You look a little peaked this morning."

I shrug. "Didn't sleep well, I guess." The sound of eggs and bacon sizzling gets my mouth watering. Dad shoots my mother another look. That's when I start worrying.

"Kids bothering you at school, son?" Dad asks.

Something about his tone is off. He isn't mad and doesn't really sound concerned. It's something else. "Just the usual stuff," I say. "Some days I wear the target on my back, other days some other kid gets it."

"Have a bad dream or something?" Dad probes.

He tries to sound casual, but I recognize the edge in his voice. Maybe that's when I *really* start worrying. Still, I'm glad he didn't ask me if I'm having girl trouble as my thoughts drift to Laura Maxwell.

"Arnie?" Dad says.

"Yeah, I think it was a bad dream." I say carefully. "But I don't really remember it."

Mom puts a plate of bacon and eggs in front of me and I set to work. But as I do, I keep one eye on my folks. Something is definitely going on. They'd been watching me extra careful for several weeks now, but this morning is even worse. The way they keep looking at each other.

"What's going on?" I cry, setting my fork down with a clatter.

"You've got yolk on your face," Mom says, reaching toward me with a napkin.

I pull my face back and take the napkin from her. "I got it." As much as I want to stare them down and wait for an answer, my stomach isn't having it. I tear back into the bacon and eggs, unable to remember ever being so hungry.

***

When the bus comes, I scurry to my usual seat and pull my hoodie on. Maybe today will be someone else's turn to get harassed. I lean my head against the window and close my eyes. That's when fragments of the dream start coming back, flashing in my head like the world's worst slide show.

I'm standing in the woods in the full dark of night, staring at the clouds sailing by the moon. It's cool, with a stiff breeze making it almost cold, but I don't feel it. I scan the woods, looking for...what? I can hear branches snapping, owls hooting, creatures of all manner skittering around. An awful pain develops in my joints. My shoulders hunch in response but I can't alleviate the ache in my elbows and hips and knees. I look down, stunned to realize I'm naked—

"Arnold," a voice whispers, pulling me from my memory...or maybe it was a dream of a dream. I open my eyes and sure enough it's Derek March leaning toward me, wearing that cocky sneer he always has no matter what the situation.

"What's up, Derek?" I say, hoping it would be one of the days I got off easy. Maybe just some name-calling or a couple dead-arm shoulder punches.

"You know what's up," he scoffs. "Remember history class yesterday? I'm sure you do, see, 'cause yesterday is sort of history now and you're so damn smart about history."

"Derek—"

He pushes my face against the window. Hard. "I failed the quiz, Arnold. Do you know why?"

I want to tell him it's because he didn't study and because he's an all-around moron, but that won't help my plight. "Mrs. Wanker was watching me like a hawk," I cry, hoping the derogatory nickname for Mrs. Shaanker will buy me some sort of reprieve. My eyes burn with tears but I realize then that I'm not really scared. No, I'm mad. Pissed off.

"That ain't good enough, Arnold," Derek croons, that shit-eating smirk still there. "You know why? Because now I got detention. And Wanker is sending a note home to my folks. You wanna know what that means?"

"No!" I say, wrenching my head free from his grasp. "I don't wanna know because I don't give a shit. I hope it means your no-good drunk of a father—" I don't even see his fist coming. It's just there, mashing my lips against my teeth, the force bouncing my head off the window. If I wasn't wearing the hood to soften the blow, it might have knocked me out.

I'm alone in the woods, naked. No, not alone. Whoever...whatever I had been searching for is there. I crouch, moving silently through the dark forest. I don't step on a single stick or rustle any branches to give myself away. Some primitive instinct has taken over as I circle around the figure in the woods. It's a man...no, just a kid, really. He stops, cocking his head as if sensing my presence. I realize I know him. Then I'm on him, tearing, biting, slashing. His screams are loud but it's the smell drives me. The sweet coppery aroma of fresh blood. I throw my head back and—

"Get off!"

Someone grabs me by the hood of my sweatshirt and jerks me backward. I crash over the seats on the other side of the aisle, tumbling in a heap onto the seat. But I'm back up in an instant, lunging toward the kid in the woods—

I stop, knowing that isn't right as arms encircle me and throw me to the floor. I land hard, and they land on top of me expelling the air from my lungs in a whooshing grunt. People are screaming and crying but I don't know why. But what I really can't figure out is why I thought Derek was some kid in the woods.

***

My father's voice comes to me from the far end of a long tunnel. "They said he was snarling, growling, trying to bite the other boy. You know what that means."

"It was a fight," my mother retorts, her voice closer. "Teenage boys are like that, aren't they?"

I open my eyes. There's no tunnel. I'm on the couch, an icepack on my head, being studied by my parents like the victim in an alien abduction movie. They both try to smile when they realize I'm awake. It's a horrible sight.

"How are you?" Mom asks, that rictus smile plastered on her face.

"I'm okay," I say, not really knowing if I am.

"Drink this," my father says, holding out a glass.

"Howard, are you sure?" Mom asks him.

Dad gives her a look and pushes the glass closer. I raise it to my lips and drink. It tastes awful, like that first metallic drink from a garden hose. As the liquid flows from the glass to my mouth, it looks like it's shimmering in the light. Maybe I'm really not okay, I think. I finish it and lie back down. My alien abductors watch me until it all goes blank.

***

I wake up to blinding sun scorching my eyes and the worst headache I can remember. And there is Mom, standing over my bed. "No school today?" I know by the angle of the sun I've way overslept the bus.

"Not today," she says. "How are you feeling?"

I gesture vaguely toward the throbbing thing on my shoulders. "Headache," I mumble, closing my eyes against the terrible light.

"Rest up, Arnie," Mom says.

I try to nod but it sends legions of pain through my skull. I moan, hoping she gets the message.

The next time I open my eyes, it's dark outside my window. It gives me an uneasy feeling. I never sleep this much. My head still hurts, and everything feels a little muddled. "At least nobody's standing over me while I'm sleeping," I mutter, trying to sit up. I gasp. There's Dad, sitting at my desk chair, smoking his pipe, and you guessed it: watching me.

"How are you, Arnie?" Dad says softly.

Dad sounds so compassionate. For some reason my mind jumps back to breakfast the day before. *Kids bothering you at school, son?* He had sounded so different, and it popped into my fuzzy brain why that was. He'd sounded hopeful, wanting that to be what was bothering me. Because it was somehow better than the dreams. "I'm not sure," I say because it's the truth. "What's happening to me?"

"It's a family condition," Dad says. "It's too much for you to hear now. When you're stronger…" His eyes flick to the window then back to me. It happens so quickly I wonder if it really happened. "In a few days I'll tell you everything you need to know." He stands and approaches the bed, placing a gentle hand on my cheek. His other hand comes out of his pocket holding a small vial. "Drink this. It will make you feel better."

I stare at the small glass tube, noticing the way the light reflects off its contents.

He shakes the vial and unscrews the cap.

I look at the liquid, the iridescent silver fragments dancing in a slowing circle. I drink the liquid, shifting my gaze to meet my father's eyes. When I'm finished, I close my eyes and lie back down. Whatever is happening is beyond my control. I have no choice but to trust my parents.

***

Monday rolls around and there's still no explanation. Just a lot of strange looks and a few more doses of the strange liquid. I'm spared the pain of the bus ride because my parents have to bring me to school and talk with the principal about the fight. It's an awkward ride, mostly silent but with a few stilted attempts at small talk.

We enter the school and walk toward the main office. The eyes that follow me are not the usual stares. These aren't kids watching the oddball kid or ogling the troublemaker on his way to the principal's office. These eyes hold fear. I keep my head down until we're in the office.

My parents chat briefly with Mrs. Granger, then principal McIntire beckons from his inner office. I stand to go but he says, "Just your folks, Arnold. Relax out here, we won't be long."

I sit as the door closes behind them. I glance at Mrs. Granger who gives me a nervous smile before going back to her computer.

I close my eyes, feeling like my headache might be trying to make a comeback. Distant voices vie for my attention. I open my eyes and stare at the door to McIntire's office. My eyes widen when I realize the voices are my parents' and Principal McIntire's. I shouldn't be able to hear them through the school's old thick walls and the heavy wooden door. But when I concentrate, I realize I can make them clearer, like I'm tuning in an old radio.

Principal McIntire: He was growling, Mr. Dubois. He tried to bite the other boy.

Dad: This boy attacked my son. He was only trying to defend himself after having his head smashed into a bus window.

Principal McIntire: Nevertheless, we cannot tolerate this type of behavior.

Mom: What of the other boy? Where are his parents?

Principal McIntire: I have a meeting with them immediately following this.

The door to the outer office opens, pulling me from the conversation. I stifle a gasp. It's Laura Maxwell, carrying a folder I assume to be for the principal.

She does a double-take when she sees me sitting there. "Oh, hi Arnie."

Her surprised smile warms my aching heart. "Hi Laura," I say, trying to return her smile.

Laura hands the folder to Mrs. Granger. "Mr. Gianni asked me to bring this to you."

Mrs. Granger thanked her. Then Laura turned to me. "I'm glad you're back," she says.

I stand, feeling silly looking up at her. "Thanks. Glad to be back." Then I add, "I guess..."

She laughs as she studies my face. "Are you okay?" She gestures toward the bruise on my forehead.

"Yeah, I'm fine." I've had a crush on Laura since the beginning of the school year. We've talked a lot and studied together a few times in the library, but I really want to be more than friends. I screw up my courage. "Laura, do you want to—"

The door from the hall bursts open and there stands Derek March, flanked by a man and woman I assume to be his parents. The man is big and beefy and mean looking. The woman looks haggard, a vacant, haunted look in her eyes. Derek glares at me, then his expression changes as he looks back and forth between Laura and me. "Arnold," he says. "And...Laura, isn't it?"

My face heats up, partly out of anger but also because of Derek seeing me talking to Laura. His sly smile sends a cold tingle down my spine. A primal dread fills me.

The door to Principal McIntire's office opens and he steps quickly between me and Derek. "Arnold, you may return to class now," he says sternly. "That goes for you as well, Miss Maxwell." I mumble a goodbye to my parents and leave the office with Laura.

"I really don't like him," Laura grumbles as we walk down the hall.

"Really?" I say. "He acted like he didn't even know you."

"We've known each other since grade school," she huffs. "He just acts like that because he knows I can't stand him, so he pretends like he doesn't know me."

"That's kinda weird," I say.

"Forget Derek," she says, turning to me. "What were you going to say before he barged in on us?"

I stop, turning to face her. There's a pinkish blush in her cheeks and I think she already knows what I was going to say. So, I say it. "Do you want to go to the dance with me?"

A smile lights her face, transforming her from pretty to beautiful in my eyes.

"Yes," she says, suddenly shy. "I would really like that."

The warning bell rings, and we say goodbye. I walk quickly to my class, steps lightened by my talk with Laura.

***

I place my fork down on the table and wait for my parents to notice me staring at them. When they do, they exchange another one of their parental looks. "I need to know what happened to me last week." It has been gnawing at me. Every night I wait for them to explain, and they never do.

My father sighs, putting his own silverware on the table. "I suppose I've put it off for as long as I can," he says.

His voice is weary, old sounding. It unsettles me. I suddenly don't care what happened to me. What *is happening* to me. I don't want to hear what he has to say.

My father says, "Have you ever heard of the loup-garou?"

I stare at him, waiting for the punchline, but his face remains somber. "The werewolf?" I ask. The hot, sick feeling in my stomach tells me the rest. But I wait and let Dad tell it.

"It is not some myth," he says. "Though it has become more folklore than fact. You...*we*..." he points to me, then himself – "are loup-garou. It is a species. Not some monster as the tales would make us out. A *species*. But a dying species."

I have no words. Even if I did, the sandpaper that was now my throat would not allow them to come.

"There are not many of us left, and the genetics are not always passed down. We don't know until a child gets to be your age. Puberty."

I recall how closely they have been watching me. Waiting. Then something else hits me. "Mom?" I croak.

She shakes her head. "No, only your father. And now, you."

I have a million things I want to ask. Like how she ended up married to such a creature – *species*, I correct myself. How he manages to keep it hidden from the world. What it actually means. All I have to go on is what I've seen in movies. But my brain is spinning too fast to articulate a single one of my questions.

"I'll tell you everything you want to know," Dad says. "A lot of what you have heard is fiction. Stories made up to scare children. Later, turned into books and movies to scare, well, everyone. The change only occurs during the moon's full cycle. Usually, three nights. Sometimes only two, sometimes as many as four. But it doesn't really matter because we've developed a way to control it."

"The liquid with the shiny things floating in it," I whisper.

Dad nods. "A chemical compound similar to silver nitrate but not poisonous to us. It prevents the change when taken in the proper dose beginning a day before the cycle and continuing through the full moon."

It all clicks into place. The fight, confusing Derek with the person in my dreams. I'm a freak. A monster. Whatever is nesting in my gut begins to slither around. The room shifts and goes blurry around the edges. I suck in a breath and let it out slowly. As much as I want to run and hide from this terrible truth, the thought of passing out and having another dream terrifies me. *How will I ever sleep again?*

As if reading my mind, my father says, "The compound will help you sleep in addition to preventing the change. The dreams I suspect have been plaguing you will lessen in intensity, perhaps even stop.

It's a relief. Not much, but something.

"I'm sorry, son." Dad says, pain etched on his face. "We were hoping you would be spared this life."

"What if I miss a dose or don't take it in time?" I recall the dreams again and wonder if they were really premonitions of some sort.

"Then you will shift. And hunt," Dad says. Then he adds, "We won't let that happen."

***

The next few weeks are…normal. I feel better knowing my situation. Despite how bad it is, I'm confident in my father's words and the knowledge that it can be controlled. I sit with my parents after dinner almost every night since they broke the news, asking questions and listening to my father's stories. Seeing him living a normal, stable life eases the burden of my secret.

Even things at school are better. Derek is given a zero-tolerance warning because of his past record.

One more fight and he will be suspended, and his case reviewed by the board for possible expulsion. While he still abuses me verbally, it is hands off. His words don't faze me anymore.

Finally, the day of the dance arrives. My anxiety has been ratcheting up as the big night approached, and the school day drags as my nerves edge toward the red zone. My first date. Somehow, I'm sure I was going to screw it up in spectacular fashion. Make a fool of myself on the dance floor. Spill punch all over Laura. Forget to wear pants. The possibilities my mind conjure grow more ridiculous as the day wears on.

***

The ride to Laura's house is awkward. Dad keeps trying to give me advice but I'm not really listening. The cycle starts tonight so I'd taken my first dose of the compound the night before. My parents tried to get me to take the second dose before we picked up Laura, but I managed to negotiate taking it after. I was nervous it was going to make me feel weird or nauseous or who knows what. The look on each of my parents' face told me all I needed to know about the seriousness of my condition, though it still seemed like nothing more than a bad dream. They finally relented, making me bring the vial with me and exacting a promise I'd take it by eleven.

We pull up to Laura's house and I get out, checking my shirt and tie for...I don't even know. Wrinkles? Stains? I'd stressed over the outfit for over an hour, time to stop worrying. I ring the doorbell and wipe my sweaty palms on the back of my pants. Mr. Maxwell opens the door somehow looking both sad and nervous.

"Come in, Arnie," he says. We shake hands and I say hi to Mrs. Maxwell.

Then Laura comes down the stairs. She's wearing a skirt and blouse, nothing Hollywood red carpet or anything, but she looks amazing. Her hair is pulled up in some sort of fancy style with ringlets framing her face. She smiles and my knees almost buckle.

"You look nice," I say, my face in flames. It's not nearly enough to convey how I think she looks but it sends a pinkish flush to her cheeks.

"You look nice, too," she says.

Her parents give us instructions about what time to be home and all that, but I barely hear any of it. All I can think of is how beautiful she looks. And wonder why she's going to the dance with me. She could be going with any guy at school.

I introduce her to my dad, and we ride in eternal awkward small talk to the school. Finally, we arrive and I escape the claustrophobic confines of the car.

The night is cool but comfortable as we walk toward the gymnasium entrance. I don't know if I should hold her hand or anything, but the problem solves itself. Our fingers brush together as we walk up the stairs and then interlace as if we've been doing it forever. I sense her glancing at me but I'm afraid to meet her gaze. The goofy smile I know is plastered on my face might send her running.

The gym is decorated in an undersea theme. I vaguely remember a survey going around but didn't realize which had won. Seahorses, sharks, octopi, and mermaids dangle from the ceiling. The lighting is bluish-green and paper mâché coral reefs are sprouting from the floor. I know it probably looks amateur and a little silly, but to me it's magical. I risk a glance at Laura and the expression on her face tells me she feels the same.

"There's Mishi," Laura says. "Let's go say hi."

Mishi is Laura's best friend. I've known her since kindergarten, but we never really became friends. She seems like a nice girl but it's just one of those things where we never traveled in the same circles. Now we do, I think.

Mishi is there with a kid named Cillian Donlevy, an Irish exchange student. I didn't know exchange students were still a thing. We stand in a circle making small talk as the gym fills up and the deejay starts to play songs meant to get people on the dance floor. Instead, the four of us make our way to the table where the Key Club is selling snacks and drinks.

We get Cokes and sit in the stands where it's quiet and we can talk. Cillian is a funny kid, regaling us with stories of Ireland. He's a bit hard to understand with his thick brogue but it only makes the stories funnier.

Something happening on the dance floor catches our attention. Angry voices and people standing still instead of dancing. Then Derek Quinn and two of his cronies push their way through the crowd. One of the teacher chaperones rushes over and has words with Derek but he just sneers and laughs and keeps walking. Then he spots me. Something in his demeanor changes. Hardens. He elbows one of his buddies and juts his chin at me. Then he saunters over, flanked by his two goons.

"Well, well, well, it looks like little Arnold is all grown up and has an actual date that doesn't require inflation." His goons snicker and they all high five each other.

"Who's this bloke?" Cillian asks, sounding cheery.

"What did you call me?" Derek says, stepping up close to Cillian.

Mishi throws up her hands. "Derek, just get lost, huh?"

Cillian takes a step back, palms up in surrender. "Whoa, ease up, mate. I don't think we've met. I'm Cillian Donlevy, here in the US from Dublin, Ireland to study."

"Well Cillian Donlevy from Dublin, I have a couple things to say. First, you talk like a fairy. Second, hanging out with Arnold is a great way to get your ass kicked.

Cillian is eyeing Derek with a sort of wary curiosity. He looks more amused than scared. Cillian waves a hand in front of his face. "Been hittin' the 'ard stuff, I see."

I hate that a kid I've just met – a kid that seems pretty cool, too – is in Derek's crosshairs just because he's talking to me. "Derek, why don't we just call a truce for the night? Another fight and we're both going to be in a lot of trouble."

He turns to face me, now stepping into my personal space. "A truce?" He pretends to mull it over, then shakes his head. "I don't think so, Arns. See, when a dog goes rabid, it needs to be put down. Based on how you attacked me on the bus, I think *you've* gone rabid. All that growling and biting." He leans in close, and I can smell booze on his breath and see murder in his eyes. "So, I'm gonna put you down."

"Everything cool here?" It's Mr. Velasquez, one of the guidance counselors. He's tall and has the lean, muscular build of an athlete. His good looks and physique make him a favorite among the female students. It's his sheer size that makes him an effective chaperone.

Derek turns and looks up at Velasquez. "Fine as frog's hair, Mr. Velasquez." He slips a tin of mints out of his pocket and pops one in his mouth, then offers an innocent smile. "Arnie here was just asking if there were any after parties when the dance is over. I was just telling him I'm sure we'll see each other later."

"Is that right," Velasquez says evenly, clearly not buying Derek's goody-two-shoes act.

"Sure, isn't that right, Arnold?" Derek stares at me trying to look hard.

Laura moves closer and squeezes my hand. I don't know what she wants me to say but something clicks inside me. Her hand in mine gives me confidence. Maybe even courage. I look hard at him, not wavering. "Sure, Derek. We'll be seeing each other *real* soon." I smile when Derek's cocky sneer fades a little, blurs into something that looks like doubt. Then, Velasquez ushers Derek and his crew away.

"What a jerk," Mishi snaps. "He gives me the creeps."

"Are you okay?" Laura asks. Her face is steeped with concern.

"Sure," I say. "Why wouldn't I be? Cillian, I'm sorry you got dragged into that."

"It's all good," Cillian says cheerfully. He turns to Mishi, "Fancy a dance?"

Mishi nods, then turns to Laura. "Isn't he dreamy?" They both giggle as they hurry toward the dance floor.

"Wanna join them?" I ask.

Laura shrugs. "I'd rather just talk if that's okay?"

We move to the stands and find a bench away from the other groups of kids hanging out there. I stare across the gym, soaking it all in. The blaring music, the gyrating bodies, the decorations…I want to remember this forever. Especially holding Laura's hand. Her beautiful eyes.

"Earth to Arnie," she says with a grin.

I turn to her, my face flushing. "Sorry, I was just thinking—"

"About what?"

Say it, I tell myself. Don't chicken out. "About what a great night it is." I gesture toward the gym. "It's really special. Mostly because you're here with me," I blurt out, before I lose my nerve.

She looks into my eyes wearing an expression I can't describe. Then we're leaning toward each other. I close my eyes as our lips touch. The kiss is over too quickly but also seems to last forever.

"I feel the same way," she whispers.

The rest of the evening flashes by in a blur of laughter and dancing. Cillian entertains us with more stories of Ireland, keeping us in stitches. I feel like Laura and I are connecting. To make it all better, there has been no sign of Derek and his goons. I suspect he did something to get himself kicked out.

The deejay plays "Last Dance" by Donna Summer, followed by the actual last dance, a slow pop song I don't recognize. Laura and I dance close and steal a couple kisses, careful not to get spotted by the chaperones. Then, it's over.

The four of us gather at the front of the gym as the building empties. "Oh, I better run to the restroom before my dad gets here," Mishi says.

"I'll go with," Laura adds, giving me a smile. "Be right back."

I make small talk with Cillian, keeping an eye out in the parking lot for my dad's car.

A few minutes later, Mishi returns. She smiles at Cillian then looks at me, a confused expression erasing her smile. "Laura not back?" I shake my head as Mishi frowns. "I thought she left before me— Oh, there's my father, I have to go, or he'll have a cow."

We exchange goodbyes and I watch Mishi and Cillian hustle toward the parking lot. When I turn back, I realize the gym is almost cleared out. *Where is Laura?* I'm about to head toward the restrooms when I spot Dad's car. I jog over to let him know I need to wait for Laura.

"Did you take the…medicine, Arnie?" He asks, glancing at the clock on the dashboard.

"No," I say, feeling the weight of the vial in my pocket. "I'll take it now. Be right back." Before he can argue, I jog back toward the gym. The night has cooled off, a stiff breeze causing me to shiver. Clouds skip by the moon and a sudden hunger hits me. It's like nothing I've ever felt before. I know what's causing it but still leave the vial in my pocket. I rush across the gym floor, noting that only the clean-up crew and the janitor, Mr. Bosley, are left.

Mr. Bosley approaches. "Time to go home, Arnie."

"I know," I say, looking wildly around. "But Laura—" I spot one of Derek's goons coming out of the men's room. "Come on!" I pull Mr. Bosley toward the restrooms.

The kid pounds on the door and yells, "We gotta go!" Derek and his other goon come out, spot Mr. Bosley, and run past us toward the exit.

Derek's face is all scratched and the other kid is running funny.

We reach the restrooms and am hit simultaneously by another surge of hunger and a sudden dread that something is terribly wrong. Another cramp hits me, nearly doubling me over. Then I realize what is wrong: Derek and the other kid had come out of the *girls'* bathroom.

I crash through the door, followed by Mr. Bosley, as another hunger pain rips at my guts. Laura is leaning against the wall. Her hair is wet and her face is starting to swell and bruise. She's cradling one arm. Her face is a portrait of pain. "Laura..." I go to her side and put an arm around her, helping her toward the door. Her feet shuffle and she stumbles but Mr. Bosley is there to help catch her. "Can you help me get her to my dad's car?"

Mr. Bosley nods, his face a mix of concern and anger.

"Laura, did they—"

"No," she says. "But I think they would have if I didn't fight them. She smiles through swollen lips. "I got one of them in the balls and mauled Derek's face pretty good. They settled for sticking my head in the toilet. I think they broke my arm."

"Sons of bitches," Mr. Bosley seethes.

I pull her tighter. "You're amazing," I tell her.

We get outside and almost plow my father over as he's coming up the steps.

"Arnie, what's going on?"

My body burns with insatiable hunger.

"Mr. Bosley, help my dad get Laura in the car." I turn to my father. "You have to get her to the hospital."

Arnie," Dad says, bewildered. "What are you going to do?"

I pull the vial out of my pocket just as I spot Derek and his friends crossing the parking lot. I smash the vial on the stairs, watching the silvery liquid shimmer like a faraway galaxy. "I'm going hunting," I growl, loping down the steps and welcoming the change coming over me.

***

The three figures reach the end of the parking lot, moving out of the harsh lights into the darkness of the woods beyond. In my old form, I'd have known they were taking the path that cuts through to their neighborhood. Now, I just know the darkness is my friend.

One of the figures turns and utters a sound that's not quite a scream. I silence him with one swipe of my claws, barely feeling the throat tearing away and the hot spray of blood that showers my face. I shove him to the ground, watching him gurgle and twitch before finally going still.

The other two stare wide-eyed, then turn to run. I take the slow one first, tackling him as my teeth rip into the back of his neck. I feel bones snap and more delicious blood flows into my mouth. I take another mouthful of his still-warm flesh, then go after the one I really want.

Derek is fast but the woods are dark. He stumbles, scrambles to his feet, flailing forward while craning his neck to see if I'm coming. The old me would have relished the fear in his eyes but it only means the hunt is almost over now. Derek falls again, rolling onto his back, palms up in either surrender or self-defense.

I loom over him, snarling and drooling, the combination of his fear-sweat and fresh blood are driving me nearly insane with hunger. There's a flash of something in his eyes. In the part of my brain that is still human, I realize he recognizes my clothes. Before he can utter my name, I'm on him.

I pin him to the ground, the long curves of my claws piercing his shoulders. He's screaming and crying and begging but I feel nothing but hunger. I snap my jaws, taking a chunk out of his chest, chewing the meat and spitting out tattered cloth from his shirt. Blood pours out copiously but his arms are pinned and he's helpless to stem the flow.

I lean in again, burying my teeth deep into the other side of his chest. My teeth scrape ribs and I bite down, snapping bones before I yank my head back. The sound of ripping flesh combine with Derek's screams. I swallow skin, bone, and muscle, then throw my head back and bay. When I look down, the gaping hole in Derek's chest is spewing blood but the flow is slowing. I watch the light in his eyes dim, then I go for the throat.

The End

Inherent
By
Candace Nola

Gasping, Anya Holt sat straight up in bed, ripped from her slumber by the sounds of screaming. Her screaming. Her hands clutched at her throat. She swallowed hard, rubbing her neck over and over, trying to reassure herself that it was still there and intact. Flashes of golden yellow eyes still lingered in her mind's eye. Bright, intelligent, hostile eyes. The snap of teeth as jaws closed on her flesh. The feel of the foamy strands of slick saliva as the snout slid across the pulsing vein in her neck, raking down her collarbone and along her jawline.

She sat shuddering. Her body was covered in goosebumps. Her heart crashed within its cage of bone as she forcibly willed herself to calm down. Inhale. Exhale. She breathed in deeply, held it, blew it out. Good, she told herself, again. Inhale. Exhale. Again. One minute passed, then two. As the third minute passed, her hands dropped from her throat, and she clasped them together against her stomach, feeling each inhalation and exhalation. Tears spilled from red-rimmed eyes and slid over the curves of her cheeks, into her hairline, and along her neck, leaving her pillow damp beneath her.

This was the third straight week of the nightmares. Always the same, always lucid, always terrifying. Anya thought she was losing her mind. She wasn't a child, for fuck's sake. She was a thirty-year-old woman with a house and a career. She definitely had not been drinking, hadn't had a drop since her birthday. She used no drugs, barely took vitamins. She ate a healthy diet. There was nothing she could think of to be causing the nightly disturbances.

She sniffed back more tears, wiping her runny nose with one hand. Angrily, she punched the empty expanse of the bed next to her with one balled up fist. Frustration. Fear. Anxiety. Tension. Crippling emotions swirled through her mind as she tried to make sense of it. Feeling small, invisible and scared, like she always had as a child, she rolled to her side, pulled her knees upward and curled herself into the fetal position. Anya shuddered a final time as she began to rock herself from side to side; Her traumatized psyche launching into old self soothing rituals to calm her body into sleeping. Minutes later, she was asleep, her slight frame barely visible beneath the blankets.
**

As the first rays of dawn crept rosy fingers across her ceiling, Anya opened her eyes, blinking rapidly at the offensive light as it fell across her face. She groaned and rolled over, burrowing into her pillow to block the sunlight. Anya laid there for a few more minutes, allowing her mind and her body time to wake. A cat-like stretch rippled through her as she yawned, arms and legs outstretched, toes curling, back arching. She swung her legs over the side of the bed as she sat up. Nothing like a good toe-curling stretch to start the day. She had almost forgotten the disturbances from the night before...almost.

Her brow furrowed as she checked her reflection in the bathroom mirror. Crimson welts carved trails along her collarbone and neck. Almost claw-like beneath the bright light over the vanity. She stared at the marks, then lifted her hands to inspect them. Scant bits of red clung to her fingernails, remnants of her panicked inspection of her throat from the nightmare that woke her.

Flashes of snarling, yellow fangs and blood spraying from the gaping wound in her neck hurtled through her mind, reminding her of how real the dream had felt. She closed her eyes for a moment, squeezing them tight. *Inhale. Exhale.* She breathed deep and slow. Again. *Inhale. Exhale.* Anya shook her head to clear it, opened her eyes, nodded at her reflection as if to say *'I'm okay now,'* and reached into the shower stall to turn the water on.

She dropped her pajamas on the floor in front of the sink, flicked the switch to turn the fan on, then stepped into the hot spray. Immediately, the tension left her shoulders and neck as she turned in a slow circle, rolling her head from side to side to loosen the knots that had burrowed there over the night. Water cascaded down her body, soothing and waking her at the same time. She took her time soaping up, washing her hair, shaving her legs and underarms. She was prone to coarse dark hair, matching the long raven strands that clung wetly to her face and back.

Her nana had said their family was all the same. Something to do with their heritage and bloodline. Anya was a pretty woman, had been an attractive girl, but the thick hair on her limbs and other areas had always bothered her. Her shower routine took a good fifteen minutes, but she relished it, especially after the night she had. When the hot water started to run cold, she shut the taps off and stepped out, wrapping herself in a soft white towel. She bent forward, letting her hair fall over her face and wrapped it with another towel, setting it loosely atop her head.

Anya left the steam-filled bathroom and padded in bare feet across the hall to her bedroom. Opening the double closet doors, she stood gazing at the racks of clothes, organized by color and season. Saturdays were easy days, so she grabbed her favorite pair of leggings and a long sleeve t-shirt, pulled heavy socks from her dresser drawer along with her underthings and sat them down on the bed, then started getting dressed for her day. Her cell phone chimed as she finished and glanced at it to see the notification.

Wendy was already texting her, barely eight in the morning, but she was ready for coffee and their walk. Anya chuckled and picked up the phone to respond.

Fifteen minutes? At Sophie's Shack? her reply message said.

Perfect! See ya there! Wendy replied almost instantly.

Anya set the phone down and hunted for her sneakers beneath the bed where she kicked them off the night before. She slipped her feet into them and stepped over to her dresser mirror to apply a light coat of foundation to conceal the dark circles under her eyes and some lip gloss to add color to pale lips.

She frowned at the red marks still visible on her neck and padded over to her closet once more. Her gray scarf hung on a hook on the inside door, so she grabbed it and tossed it around her neck, wrapped it twice, then let the scarf hang loose. Her jacket went on next, then she grabbed her crossbody bag, slung it on and retrieved her phone.

A minute later, Anya was outside her front door, skipping down her steps and headed down the block to meet Wendy at their favorite coffeehouse on the corner.

**

"So, you woke up clawing at your throat again?" Wendy asked, pulling Anya's scarf aside to look at the marks on her neck. The fresh marks were a bright red, in stark contrast to the faded lines beneath from nights past. Their coffee sat between them on the small table in the corner, all but forgotten as Anya recounted the nightmare. Wendy let the scarf fall and sat back in her chair, concern etched on her pretty face.

Anya stared out the window for a minute, then down at her mug, stirring it idly as she let Wendy gather her thoughts.

"I mean, maybe it's time to see someone about this? I know you're not into therapy but the same dream, for weeks on end?" Wendy said, "You're losing sleep. You're hurting yourself. You look like hell, Anya, and I mean that with love. I'm worried about you."

"I know, but it's a just a dream, right?" Anya shrugged, "how silly would I look going to a therapist about a dream?"

"Not silly at all, hun. Sometimes, dreams do mean something and sometimes they're more than a dream. Maybe it's an old memory or something you heard in your childhood. Maybe you just need to discover where it's coming from, and it'll help you resolve it."

"Yea, maybe you're right." She shrugged. "I'll ask Nana first, see if she remembers telling me about any scary stories like that or something weird that I forgot."

"That's a plan. Can't hurt to talk to her about it." Wendy smiled and nodded. "My grandma has been my therapist since I was twelve."

"Nothing like Grandma Tilly's cookies and cocoa." Anya smiled at her friend, a montage of fond memories flooding her like it was yesterday. She and Wendy had spent many days after school gathered in Grandma's Tilly's homey kitchen, eating cookies, doing homework and talking about everything from mean teachers to cute boys. She felt the same about her Nana and if anyone would know what the dreams might mean or where they came from, it would be her.

"Well, that's settled then. Nana's house first thing tomorrow. I'll drive you there myself. Today, we shop!" Wendy declared, swallowing the last of her coffee and pushing Anya's cup toward her. "Drink up. You need it and you need a day out."

Anya chuckled, picked up her mug and drank the last of her dark roast. The girls rose from their seats, gathered their things and headed out into the morning, ready to hit the shops. Anya smiled to herself as she followed Wendy outside. Her best friend since childhood, Wendy always knew what she needed exactly when she needed it.

Maybe Wendy was right, though. Maybe she did need to talk to a professional about this. She was truly exhausted and, if she were really honest, she was also a little scared. She would start with Nana, if for no other reason than to delay talking to a professional. Nana, at least, would make her feel better about taking that next step. And for Anya, it was as good of a starting point as any.

She waved at Sophie as they left the shop, leaving the bell over the door jingling in their wake. Anya breathed in the fresh air. Warm sunshine mingled with the scent of roses, English lavender, and cinnamon pastries as they left the café. She pushed the darkness from her mind, for now. It could wait a day. Today, she would shop with Wendy. She would laugh. She would smile. She would feel normal, even if only for a few hours.

***

Anya practically fell through her apartment door that afternoon when she arrived home, bags hanging from both arms and her purse slung over her shoulder. She stumbled to the couch and dropped the bundles, giggling as she did so. Wendy followed her in, equally loaded down with purchases. The girls sank into opposite corners of the couch, laughing as several bags toppled to the floor.

"What a day!" Wendy said, leaning her head back and staring at the ceiling before rolling her head toward Anya.

"Pizza?" She grinned.

"Always." Anya replied. "Your turn to pay, though."

"I'm on it." Wendy said, sinking deeper into the couch, "Soon as I get my second wind."

"You do that. I gotta pee," Anya said, groaning as she stood up once more. Her feet ached, but in a good way. They had shopped and walked the day away. She needed it. The sunlight, the fresh air, the conversations about all things silly and ridiculous. Too much coffee, way too many samples of baked goods and chocolates, just a perfect day. Exactly what the doctor ordered.

She chuckled as Wendy stretched like a cat and walked from the room, ambling down the hallway toward the bathroom. She heard more bags topple and a faint curse word from Wendy, whom, Anya assumed, failed to catch the bags before they crashed to join the rest on the carpet.

She flicked the light switch on the wall and jumped back with a cry as two glowing eyes flashed at her from the mirror. She backed out of the room, nearly slamming into the wall as the eyes vanished as quickly as she had seen them.

"You alright?" Wendy called from the living room.

"Umm, yeah. Yes, I'm fine. All good." Anya called back, peeking her head into the bathroom once more.

It looked normal and empty now. No eyes, no dark reflection. Nothing. She stepped back inside, peering around every corner. Nothing but white walls, cabinets, a toilet and mirrored glass doors enclosing the shower stall. A few light touches of bright pink and gold added some pops of color, but nothing that would have caused that reflection.

"Get your shit together, Anya," she muttered to herself as she closed the door and went to the toilet to relieve herself. Her bladder was screaming at her by this point. It almost hurt to sit down, and she was gushing urine almost before she finished sitting on the cold porcelain.

She finished, sat there for a minute longer staring at the mirror, perplexed and still a bit shaken. She wiped and stood, pulled her panties up along with her leggings, and went to wash her hands. Again, her eyes were drawn to the depths of the mirror. She stared at her reflection and of the bathroom behind her, taking in every object that showed itself in the mirror.

Nothing could have been what she saw. She saw eyes. Two glowing eyes. Had she been in court, she would have sworn it on the Bible. Anya sighed, dried her hands, and left the bathroom, leaving the light on behind her.

"Hey, umm slumber party?" She said when Wendy glanced at her as she walked back into the room.

"Sure, but I'm stealing your clothes." Her friend replied, chuckling. "I'm always game for a sleepover."

Anya stopped short, pausing by the couch. She looked for the pile of chaos that had been on the floor, but nothing was there. She turned and saw that Wendy had put most of their shopping away. Fruit sat in the basket on the table. The bottles of wine were on the counter next to the fridge. Her bag and jacket were hung on the hooks next to the front door, Wendy's coat and purse next to her own.

"Hey, you didn't have to do that..." she said gratefully as she sank down on the couch. She curled her feet up beside her and watched Wendy browse the movie channels on the television.

"Well, I got bored, so I ordered the pizza, put your clothes in your room and put the groceries away." Wendy glanced at her again, "you sure you're okay?"

"Yes, I'm fine," Anya replied, looking at her with an eyebrow raised. "Why do you keep asking?"

"Because you were gone almost fifteen minutes," Wendy said. "I thought maybe you had gotten sick."

"What?" Anya said, staring at Wendy until she looked over at her. "I just peed, like, I was gone two minutes, if that."

Wendy was shaking her head before Anya finished speaking.

"No, you were gone almost fifteen minutes. I've watched at least a dozen videos on my phone and put all the stuff away."

"But…" Anya trailed off. "I thought I saw something…but maybe I got lost in thought trying to figure out what it was."

"Saw what?" Wendy said, all business now, remote discarded on the coffee table. "Tell me."

"I'm not sure really, probably just a trick of the light, but they looked so real…" Anya said, talking more to herself than Wendy as her voice trailed off. The image flashed in her mind again, and she shuddered.

"Anya, what did you see?

"Eyes." Anya said. "Two glowing eyes."

"Eyes?"

She nodded, waiting for her friend's reaction.

"Animal eyes? Human eyes?"

"Animal, I think," Anya said. "But maybe not. They seemed intelligent somehow, like not quite human, but more than just an animal."

Wendy nodded, waiting for more.

"That's all." Anya shrugged. "I stepped in, went to switch the lights on. Two golden eyes flashed right at me from the mirror and then they were gone, right when the lights turned on. I yelped, jumped back, and then when I went back in, there was nothing there."

"That's what the noise was," Wendy said. "I knew I heard something."

"I'm sure it was just a weird reflection." Anya shrugged, then leaned forward and snagged the remote from the table.

"What are we watching?" she asked, closing the discussion in her typical fashion. Wendy snorted and stood up as her phone pinged, signaling the arrival of the pizza.

"Saved by the bell, for now." Wendy said. "You pick. I chose the pizza."

"Did you put olives on it?" Anya asked, frowning and rolling her eyes when Wendy chuckled as she went to the door.

"Damnit."

"Hey, you snooze, you lose," Wendy said.

"What in the world did you get?" Anya asked, as Wendy came back with the food.

"Well, I got pizza for me. And pizza for you. And wings. And breadsticks."

"There's only two of us," Anya chuckled. She rose and padded over to the kitchen to get the wine and two bottles of water.

"So?" Wendy clearly didn't see the problem. "It's movie and pizza night, just like the old days at Grandma Tilly's."

"Clearly. Guess it's Leatherface first," Anya said, grinning as Wendy plopped down on the floor, her customary spot on movie nights. She started dishing up food as Anya turned the movie on.

**

Hours later, Wendy woke up confused and disoriented. Noises she couldn't place were coming from somewhere beside her. She opened her eyes and looked around, taking a second to remember that she was at Anya's. Wild movement next to her startled her, and she turned toward Anya, seeing her gasping and thrashing; both hands were clutched to her neck, scraping and digging into the flesh. Her mouth opened and shut, teeth snapping together with a harsh click, as if she were biting something.

Wendy sat up immediately, her heart pounding in her chest.

"Anya! Hey, Anya, wake up! It's a dream! Just a dream!" She reached for her friend, attempting to put a hand on her shoulder to rouse her, but Anya's jaw snapped at her as if by instinct. Her eyes flashed open, hostile and glowing like a sunset, and a deep snarl emitted from her throat. Wendy slid backwards, falling off the edge as she backed away in fear from the feral thing on the bed. Anya barely looked like herself, shrouded by black shadows and the skeletal glow of the moon. Her face looked elongated and dark. Her eyes seemed sunken and eclipsed by a heavy brow. Everything about the woman she knew looked bestial and wrong. Terror gripped her.

"Anya!" Wendy yelled, panic in her voice. "Wake up! You're dreaming! Goddamnit, Anya, Wake up!" She cried out, tears spilling from her eyes as Anya snarled and thrashed and clawed her own neck. Wendy reached for the lamp in the corner, yanking the chain and turning the light on. Warm amber flooded the room and Anya's body sat straight up, her eyes opening wide and her hands dropping from her neck. She heaved, great gasping sobs as she frantically looked around the room, finding Wendy huddled in the corner.

"What happened? Are you okay?"

"You were dreaming again, a bad one." Wendy said, not moving from the corner. "I've never seen you like that."

Anya blinked at her friend; her brow furrowed as she studied her. Wendy was still shaking as she hesitantly came toward the bed.

"Are you okay?" She asked, standing near the foot of the bed. Fear was evident on her face as she looked at Anya and the oozing gouges on her neck. "You almost bit me and your eyes got all...funny." Wendy continued, almost sheepishly. "You clawed yourself again, too. Looks worse this time."

"What?" Anya gasped; her eyes wide as Wendy's words sunk in. "I'm so sorry. I don't know why this is happening. Are you okay?"

"I'm fine. Just freaked out a bit more than normal. Our sleepovers can get pretty wild, but tonight will go down in history." Wendy chuckled, relaxing and walking from the room. "Sit tight. I'll get you a washcloth for those scratches."

Anya watched her leave the room, then looked at her hands. Bloodstains covered her fingers and palms. Bits of tissue were stuck beneath her nails. She swallowed and felt the burning on her neck as if the pain was waiting for her to be more awake before making itself known. Her neck radiated heat. Tears filled her eyes as Wendy walked back into the room, a dripping washcloth in her hands.

Anya began to sob as Wendy sat beside her. She held her best friend as she sobbed, utterly spent and confused as to what was happening to her and why. Wendy rocked her like Nana used to, stroking her hair until she was cried out.

"Nana's first thing in the morning. We need to figure this out." Wendy said as she began to clean Anya's wounds when she calmed down.

Anya nodded and sat quietly, letting Wendy take care of her, as always.

***

Morning was a sober affair as the girls got ready for the trip to Nana's house. An hour's ride from the city, Nana lived in a small rural town, in the same house that Anya had grown up in. It was the kind of town where everyone knew everyone. Their kids had gone to school together, had little league games together, and backyard cookouts. Anya's father had been raised there.

He had married her mother there in the backyard and they had all lived there until Anya's mother died during a camping trip. After that, her father had succumbed to grief and depression, after pretending to fight it for months for Anya's sake. Eight months after Anya's mother had died, her father had vanished into the night, leaving her with Nana and a single letter. Anya was left with a broken heart, alone in the world, at four years old.

"Almost ready?" Wendy asked her, watching her from across the room.

"Huh?" Anya looked at her, startled, pulling herself from her thoughts. "Oh, yes. Just let me pour another cup." She held up her travel mug to Wendy in a mock salute and nodded at the coffeepot that was still brewing. "It's almost ready."

"Oh good, refill mine too?" Wendy said, coming over and putting her cup down on the counter. "I'm gonna put my shoes on. Do you need anything else before we go?"

"Nope, all good. Got my stuff on the couch."

Wendy glanced at her from her seat on the couch where she plopped down to tug her shoes on. "Want me to get your scarf?" She asked, her voice a bit quieter than before.

Anya's hand rose to her neck and touched the soft bandages that Wendy had applied to her wounds the night before.

"Oh, yes, please. I don't want to scare Nana."

"On it." Wendy yanked on her other shoe, adjusted her socks and pants, and stood. "Back in a jif." She smiled at Anya and bounced down the hallway, doing her weird half-jog, half-skip thing that she had been doing since grade school. Wendy rarely walked like a normal person. Her energy practically vibrated from her body. Anya smiled, watching her go and felt almost normal for the first time all morning.

***

Settled in the car, Anya relaxed in the passenger seat as Wendy pulled her compact car onto the road. A few minutes of silence followed while Wendy navigated the streets through town to the highway. Anya fiddled with her playlist and attached her phone to Wendy's radio, letting the music filter through the car speakers.

Sunshine beamed overhead. The morning was beautiful, bright blue sky, clean and clear as far as the horizon stretched. Anya loved days like this. She felt like she lived for the sunshine. She rolled the window down and let the air rush in. Finally, Wendy spoke.

"Do you want to talk about it?"

"Don't know what more to say, honestly." Anya sighed. "Just want to see what Nana says. It's gotten scarier after last night, and I'm so sorry I scared you."

"Hey, I'm fine. Sure, it freaked me out, but I'm also glad I was there to stop you from hurting yourself worse. I knew it was bad, but now that I've seen it, you have someone that can back you up, you know?"

Anya nodded, a thoughtful look on her face. "That's true. I didn't think of that. I suppose some folks will wonder if it's as bad as I'm saying or wonder if I'm making it up."

"You damn sure are not making it up." Wendy snorted. "I can vouch for that."

Wendy looked at Anya, patted her leg. "It'll be fine. No harm, no foul. Remember that time you pushed me off the swings in fifth grade?"

Anya laughed. "Yes, and I still feel awful about it."

"Yea, but that was worse than any little bite mark you would have left on me." She chuckled. "You may have been dreaming that you're a beast, but you're still just little Anya to me."

"Thanks. Knew I could count on you to keep me grounded," Anya replied, smiling at her and tuning the music up a bit.

"Okay, okay. Point taken." Wendy said, "Let's save it for Nana."

The next forty minutes passed easily as the girls sang along to the music and laughed over other memories that they shared of making this same trip countless times in their lives. Anya was grateful for the conversation, but her anxiety grew, settling like a boulder in her gut.

When Wendy pulled the car off the main highway and turned onto the two-lane road leading to Nana's, the conversation grew quiet. The atmosphere in the car turned somber and Anya felt her stress grow until it felt like she might burst.

"Hey, hun. Breathe." Wendy said, glancing at her, alarm on her face and concern in her voice. "You're practically purple."

Anya looked startled, then gasped for air, breathing in quickly, embarrassed. She felt her face flush and the gouges on her neck burned fire.

"You okay?" Wendy asked as she parked the car in front of Nana's.

"I'm okay. Just got nervous, think I zoned out there for a minute. Just worried about what Nana might say." Anya said quietly, staring at the small cottage with its welcoming wrap-around porch, flanked by multi-colored flowerbeds and a stone pathway. Weeping willow trees lined the side yard and Anya's old tire swing still hung from one of the thick branches.

"Place looks great," Wendy said. "Ready?"

Just as she asked, the porch door opened, and an elegant woman stood in the doorway. Gray hair, done up in an elegant bun, framed a pretty face. Soft gray eyes watched them, and a cheerful smile blossomed beneath rosy cheeks. She wore a loose gray sweater and black jeans. A pair of slippers adorned her feet.

"She's just lovely as ever." Wendy said, opening her door. Anya followed suit, and the girls exited the car and went to greet the old woman watching them.

***

Nana's first words stunned both girls into silence as they gathered around her kitchen table like they had when they were girls.

"I've been waiting for you." Nana sighed. She stared right at Anya as she spoke, studying her. "Have the dreams started? I can tell you're not sleeping. You look like hell."

Nana looked at Wendy, "And you, are you taking care of her? How long has it been happening?"

"Wait, what?" Anya stammered, "What do you mean you've been waiting for me? And how do you know about the dreams? What is going on, Nana?"

"And if you knew, why the hell didn't you tell her earlier?" Wendy demanded. Her tone was serious, but her expression was more concern than anger.

"Don't take that tone with me, young woman. You may be family, but you are still speaking to an elder." Nana said, scolding her gently. "I had hoped it would skip her, that's all." Nana said softly. "An old woman can hope, can't she?"

"Nana, please tell me what's going on," Anya said. "I'm scared."

"I'm sure you are, dear. I was too, when it first happened to your father." Nana sighed. "Right after he turned thirty."

Anya and Wendy shared a look, then looked at Nana, who just looked sad. "Like I said, I've been waiting for you. I hadn't heard anything from you, so I grew hopeful, but yet, here you are, so I guess I was wrong."

The girls waited, silently urging her to continue. The old woman sighed, stirring her tea as she gazed into the dark liquid. The grandfather clock behind her clicked away as the moment stretched on. She lifted her head to look at them.

"Before I continue, I need you to promise to listen to the entire story. You need to understand that things were done to protect you, things you may not understand. You may be angry when I explain, and you may be hurt but I need you to listen. Can you do that?"

Nana's eyes were piercing as she spoke, boring holes directly into Anya's soul. Anya swallowed and nodded.

"Take that scarf off. Let me see," Nana ordered.

Anya did as she was told, and Nana rose from her seat and gently removed the bandages. She made a quiet 'tsking' sound in her throat as she saw the oozing trails of blood running down Anya's throat.

"Wendy. You are a part of this now. If you are here, you already know too much." Nana looked at the other girl. "Do you understand that whatever happens from here on out cannot be shared with anyone else? It's to keep her safe. Hell, it's to keep us all safe."

"I understand, Nana. I just want to help her with whatever this is." Wendy said.

"Alright. Let's go to the other room then. Might as well get comfortable." Nana said. She stood and lifted the tray of cookies from the middle of the table. "Bring your tea, girls. It's going to be a long day."

Anya and Wendy shared a look as they did as they were told and followed Nana from the kitchen. Anya's heart crashed against her ribs. That leaden ball of stress grew ever larger in her stomach. Dread consumed her and suddenly, she didn't want to hear whatever Nana had to say. Fear was eating her from the inside.

They followed Nana to the sunroom in the rear of the cottage. Family pictures hung on every wall above the windows. Knick-knacks and keepsakes of all kinds littered every available surface, mixed in with the many figurines of wolves and dogs that Nana collected. Anya loved this room as a child. It was peaceful, filled with memories, and always seemed to be the heart of the house. It looked over the expansive backyard that led into the forest. Nothing but trees, trails, and mountains as far as one could go once you left the safety of the yard.

Nana had spent many nights here after Anya's father had left, watching the shadows swirling among the trees. Listening to the sounds of the night, watching the wind blow and rain fall. She sat here watching the seasons change, holding Anya on her lap, comforting her in the aftermath of what her life had become. Anya found it fitting that she would choose to deliver whatever news she had to share today, here in this room, as she had done so many times before.

Wendy and Anya got settled on the oversized couch and Nana took one of the plush wingback chairs across from them after setting the tray on the table between them.

"Nana, whatever this is, I'm sure I can handle it myself. There's no need to bring up any painful memories if you don't want to." Anya spoke rapidly. Her fear rushing from her in words that tripped over one another in a flood, eager to stop whatever was coming.

Nana shook her head sadly. "My dear girl, you don't understand, but you will."

"But—" Anya trailed off as Nana leaned forward, taking her hands in her small, wrinkled ones.

"It'll be okay. I just need you to trust me," Nana said. "Can you do that?"

Anya swallowed hard and nodded. Wendy patted her back.

"Let's begin, then." Nana looked at them, concern and compassion in her eyes. "Your father isn't dead or missing."

Anya felt the words drop into the room like a lead balloon. A chill washed over her like ice water had just been splashed on her from the coldest depths of the ocean.

"What—" she began, but Nana shook her head.

"The story doesn't start there, though, but your story does." Nana sighed, a weary sound that seemed to issue from her very soul, not just her lungs.

"There is no other way to say this other than just say it. You are more than what you think you are. You carry your father's bloodline, a line that goes back centuries and links continents. Your heritage is one fraught with much bloodshed and many secrets. His family, our family, comes from the old country. A very old country that became Romania, long ago." Nana paused for breath.

The silence in the room was deafening and Anya felt faint. Wendy reached for her hand and squeezed it. She wanted to scream, to run, to yell out that this was all nonsense, but something tinged within her, something that told her it was all true. Her blood ran cold as her grandmother began again.

"You're changing." She told Anya bluntly. "It happens when you turn thirty. It happened to your father, but he didn't know it would. I failed him. I failed them both."

Anya saw the tears in her eyes, saw her lip tremble. Nana's hands fell to her lap, and she clasped them together to stop them from shaking.

"Your mother..." Nana said. Her voice broke, and she trailed off, swallowed, tried again. "She...It was an accident. They went camping out there along the trails to celebrate his birthday. He changed, suddenly. She never had a chance. He didn't know...I thought...I hoped it would pass him. That it would skip a generation. Sometimes it does, but it didn't. Not that time, and not now."

Anya watched a single tear fall from her grandmother's eye. Cold dread consumed her. Anger was rising in her blood. She felt hot and cold at the same time. Something within her tingled and writhed, her guts roiled. Something was off. Whatever this was, it couldn't be what she was hearing. Her grandma was older, maybe senile, maybe not saying what she meant to say clearly. Her brain swirled with thoughts. Too many to count, too many to track.

"Nana, what exactly are you saying?" Wendy asked quietly. Her face had grown pale. She was leaning forward, staring intently at the older woman. Her eyes locked onto Nana's face. The truth of what she was saying stared back. Wendy felt sick.

She, too, had been wondering if the old woman was confusing stories with reality, jumbling her thoughts from grief and loss into one strange tale, but her eyes were sharp. They dared her to argue. She sat back, shrinking into the corner of the couch, but kept hold of Anya's hand.

"I think you both know." Nana said calmly. "Look around you, Anya. Look well. I know you know what you are."

Anya stared at her, turned to see Wendy watching her, then let her gaze drift around the room. Static flooded her mind as images came into focus. Statues. Pictures. Figurines. Serious faces. Dark woods in the moonlight. Golden eyes shimmering in the frames. Wolves, everywhere. So many wolves.

Open jaws, snarling, wide maws. Glistening fangs. Those eyes, the ones from the mirror. The same as those that watched her now from the woods beyond the house. She felt it. She refused to turn around. The hairs on the back of her neck rose.

"No..." she whispered. "It's not possible. Those things don't exist. Can't exist..." Her brain recoiled, tried to shut down. The static roar of the ocean pulsed in her eardrums. She felt faint.

"Yes. It can and does. You can feel him, can't you? I knew the moment you felt him." Nana said. "He's out there. Just beyond our sight. He's been there since the night he left, watching over you from the forest. He left so he couldn't hurt you, too."

"What are you saying?" Wendy asked. "I don't understand."

"Yes, you do. Don't be foolish." Nana said to her. "I know you understand, but do I need to show you? Does she? Have you not seen enough? It's inherited through the bloodlines, passed on from firstborn to firstborn. There is no escaping it."

"But—"

"She's saying he's a wolf, Wendy." Anya said slowly, not looking at her friend. "That *we* are wolves."

"Well, you can't be a wolf," Wendy scoffed, almost relieved at the absurdity of what was being said. Her brain immediately refused to accept what she knew to be true. Human instinct kicked her, making her unable to accept what society had deemed lore and legend. "that would make you a—"

"--a werewolf." Nana finished quite bluntly. "Yes. They are werewolves, from a long line of werewolves. Anya is the firstborn. She is changing, as is the custom for her lineage. The next full moon, her transformation will be complete."

Anya's world turned gray, then dropped to black as her brain shut down, attempting to protect her from her broken reality. Wendy gasped as Anya went limp beside her. Nana stood quickly and moved toward her. Wendy had her arms around her before she could fall from the couch, but Nana pulled her away. Heat radiated from Anya's body. Her skin was red and sweat beaded on her brow.

"It's not safe. She's in shock and it could force the change. Move away and let me." Nana said, not unkindly as she sprang into action. "Go fetch a cold cloth from the kitchen."

Wendy rose and rushed from the room as Nana shifted Anya's body to a better position on the couch. She was scared and confused. Things like this didn't happen. Couldn't happen. But hadn't she seen Anya's eyes herself? Hadn't she seen the twisted visage of her face snarling in the dark just last night?

If werewolves were real, was everything else real too? Her brain refused to accept it. It was all too much to even consider. Right now, Anya needed her. She focused on the task at hand, never pausing when a sudden snarling filled the room behind her.

***

A couple of hours later, Anya woke with a start. She felt wrong. The bed felt weird, too. She groaned and rolled to her side, but found nothing there when she reached for the lamp. She forced one eye open and realized she was still at her grandmother's house, curled up in the corner of the sunroom. It was shrouded in shadows. Wendy and Nana were nowhere to be found.

"Wendy?" Anya called out, "Nana?" No response came. She pushed herself upright and winced as the movement made everything hurt. Her skin felt clammy, slick with sweat, and something else, something sticky and tacky. She called for Wendy again as she rose to her feet. Something squelched beneath her as she stood.

Fear began to snake through her mind as she made her way to the doorway to turn the light on. The carpet felt soggy. The cottage was silent, too silent. Anya flicked the light on and blinked rapidly as her eyes focused. When she turned around, she began to scream.

Blood painted the walls. It dripped from the ceiling and pooled on the floor. The furniture was splattered with it. Body parts were scattered as far as Anya could see. Nana and Wendy had been slaughtered while Anya was unconscious. The lamps on the side tables were shattered. The couch and chairs were saturated with her grandmother's remains. Most of Wendy lay in pieces near the doorway to the kitchen. She stumbled across the room, one hand over her mouth to stifle her screams. She froze as she passed the broken windows, catching her reflection in the fragmented glass.

Crimson covered her from head to toe. Violent rings of red lined her mouth, ran down her chin and collarbone and beyond. Bits of gore stained her face and stuck in her blood-soaked hair. Clumps of organs and tissue clung to her naked body. She looked around the room, shock filling her as understanding dawned. Her clothes lie in shreds across the floor.

An agonized wail broke free and turned into a howl as her jaw elongated and her fangs burst free from her mouth. A deep shudder ran through Anya as her true nature erupted. Fire ran through her veins as fury took over. Bones popped and reformed. Her body collapsed on the floor, and she writhed in agony. Hair ruptured through her pores, covering her body with thick black fur. Her nails lengthened into gleaming onyx razor blades. Anya's body shifted and shuddered as the inherent trait within her came alive.

Another howl of rage tore from her throat as she got to her feet. Her new form heaved and rippled with anger and pain. Her yellow eyes glimmered like fire in the darkness as she burst through the back door beneath the pale light of the pregnant moon. There was only one place for her to go now. One man that started all of this, the man that carried the dominant trait that had sealed her fate. He waited somewhere out there in those woods beyond the cottage, hiding behind the trees, and his own cowardice. And there would be hell to pay when she found him.

The End

Beware the Moon
By
Graeme Reynolds
A High Moor Story

11th June 1987. Monte Baldo. Italy. 23:15.

Connie grunted in pain and rubbed her swollen ankle as she gazed at the twinkling lights of Malcesine far below her. The cable car journey up the mountain had seemed like a great idea at the time, as had Steve's suggestion to walk back down the mountainside along what had appeared to be a well-worn track. The town had seemed so close, and the view had been spectacular – the castle looming above the pretty little town, with the azure blue of Lake Garda glistening in the background. There had been a cooling breeze on the mountain, which was a welcome change from the sweltering heat and humidity of the town, so she had agreed, thinking that it would make for a pleasant afternoon.

"Me and ma big mouth," she grumbled. They had made it almost halfway down the slope, and what had started as a track had become rocky and indistinct – more akin to a goat track than an actual path. Given that Connie had been wearing daps, it really should not have surprised her that she'd stumbled on the precipitous descent. Or, when she tried to stand again, a sharp pain shot through her ankle, and she'd fallen back onto the rocks once more. Steve had told her to stay where she was and had gone for help. That had been more than four hours ago.

"There is no way ah'm spending all sodding night on this mountain!" she announced to no one in particular. The ground retained the day's heat for a while, but the temperature was dropping, and her light summer clothing would do little to warm her when the night set in. If Steve wasn't coming back with help, she'd have to try to make it down herself. She steadied herself against a large granite boulder and managed to get into a one-legged standing position. Wincing, Connie put a little weight on her twisted ankle, crying out as the sharp pain lanced through her nerves. She tried again, feeling the pain return. Connie bit her lip and put more pressure on the injured leg, feeling the agony, embracing it as she fought back the tears until it seemed almost bearable. She lifted the leg and put it down again, and yes, while it still hurt like blazes, she thought that if she was careful and took it slowly, she might be able to continue. It had to be better than freezing to death. If it came to it, she'd shuffle down the track on her arse. One thing she was sure of - she wasn't waiting here for another damn minute.

The journey was more challenging than she'd imagined. Every misstep sent white-hot daggers of agony into her nerve endings. Every loose stone that shifted under her feet threatened to send her plummeting down the mountainside. Connie was under no illusions. She was in dire trouble here, and one error could actually kill her. Her thoughts turned to Steve.

What the hell had taken him so long? Had he hurt himself by rushing down the slope too quickly? Was he, even now, trying to organise a rescue party? Or was the bastard sitting in a bar with a cold bottle of Peroni? *No*, she decided. Steve wouldn't do something like that. He was probably frantic with worry right now, trying to coax some life into lethargic Italian policemen to come and rescue her. No doubt she'd meet them on the way down.

She paused to catch her breath by an ancient, long-dead olive tree, its twisted branches bleached almost white by the sun. A thought occurred to her, and Connie reached up to a low-hanging branch, grabbed hold, and pulled. A loud crack resonated across the mountain, and she almost lost her balance as the branch snapped off in her hands. It only took her a moment to wedge the thinner end between two boulders, snapping it off to create a makeshift crutch for herself. The "v" between two branches was the perfect height to rest beneath her arm, allowing her to take most of the weight off her injured ankle. She smiled despite her predicament. This should, in theory, make her journey down the mountainside less painful — perhaps even faster.

The lights of the town seemed closer now. Connie imagined that she could hear the music from the tavernas. She paused to catch her breath and listened. Yes, there was the faintest hint of music in the air — a bass beat carried to her, faint and indistinct — like a fading heartbeat. Just hearing other people — the noise of civilisation, gave her encouragement. It may take her a little longer, but she was making definite progress. She chided herself for not starting the descent sooner. Then she noticed something else. Or rather – the lack of anything else. Connie had become attuned to the noises of the mountain over the last few hours. Her only companions on the painful journey were the steady chirping of cicadas and the distant bleating of mountain goats. Now, however, everything had fallen silent, as if the mountain itself were holding its breath in anticipation. Connie felt the first real stirrings of fear in her stomach. Something was wrong here. Something was very wrong, indeed.

That was when she heard the howl.

An icy finger of terror ran down her spine, and her stomach flipped. What the hell was that? Were there wolves in Italy? Connie tried to slow her breathing and calm her shredded nerves, straining her eyes to locate the source of the howl. *It's probably someone's dog*, she told herself. *Would a wolf come this close to a town? Don't they only attack when they're hungry? Sound travels further at night – especially high up. It could be miles away. It's probably more scared of me than ah am of it. Oh shit, oh shit, oh shit!*

The mountainside was illuminated in a cool monochrome, and Lake Garda stretched out below her – a flat, ebony expanse reflecting the silver glimmering of the full moon. Full moon? The immortal lines from one of her favourite movies sprang unbidden into Connie's mind. Keep to the path. *OK... she might not have quite managed that one.* Stay off the moors. *Did a mountain count?* Beware the moon. *Shit. Stop it. Yer just making it worse. There's no such thing as werewolves. They're only in the films. Ye'll get off this damn mountain, find Steve, and have a good laugh about it. But first – ah have to get off the damn mountain!*

Connie began her descent once more, her eyes wide and her ears straining to pick up any indication that she was not alone on the desolate slopes. However, she could only hear the distant bass thump of music and the steady thud of her heart. The track became less precipitous, and consequently, the going became a little easier. Soon she would reach the vineyards and olive groves on the outskirts of the town. She felt some of the tension begin to drain out of her.

Then the howl came again. This time from directly behind her. She spun around in terror and saw the dark silhouette of something massive rise up behind her. It reminded her of a stuffed grizzly bear that she'd once seen. The creature was easily seven feet tall. While the moon shone from behind it, masking its features in stark shadows, the power and savagery emanating from the monstrous thing was palpable. It was barely ten feet away from her, and running was not an option with her injured ankle. It would be on her before she could take two steps. The beast howled again, confirming Connie's worst fears. This was no bear. No wild animal. It was something that should not exist. Could not exist.

Her heart raced, and the edges of her vision

darkened. Her limbs felt heavy, as if lead diving weights had been strapped to her wrists and ankles. The werewolf tensed, its muscles bunching. Time slowed to a crawl as Connie's fight-or-flight response kicked into overdrive and, as flight was not an option, that only left her with one alternative. The werewolf hurled itself into the air, vicious talons slashing through the air. She felt the air displaced as they swept past her – could smell the fetid, charnel stench of its breath. Connie stood poised on the brink of life and death. She swung her makeshift crutch at the beast as hard as she could. It connected with the monster's head in a satisfying crack that made her hands go numb and shattered the wood into pieces. She found herself clutching a long, sharp wooden dagger and, for a moment, allowed herself a sardonic laugh. She would be perfectly armed if she'd been facing a vampire right now. Her counter-attack had bought her only a momentary respite, but she knew that was all it was. Already it seemed to be shaking off the effects of her assault. She didn't want to die. Didn't want to be torn to pieces on a mountainside by this thing. She was supposed to be on holiday, for Christ's sake!

With the last of her strength, she threw herself forward into the attack and drove the wooden stake into the werewolf's back. The monster screamed in rage and pain, lashing out in a frenzy as it tried to reach the branch impaling it. One of the talons connected with Connie before she was able to get clear, her injured ankle slowing her down. Her back exploded in a white-hot blaze of agony before she tumbled down the screed slopes. She eventually came to rest by a large granite boulder, every nerve in her body aflame with pain. She had no idea whether she had broken any bones or how badly the werewolf's claws had injured her. Her back felt like it was on fire, and she didn't need a medical degree to work out what the warm, sticky liquid was that she felt soaking through the tattered remains of her top. Everything hurt. She'd never been in this much pain in her entire life, but she knew she had to get away. Staying where she was would mean a very painful, very messy death at the hands of the beast. She winced, biting down on her lip once more as she tried to force herself into a crouching position. Then, using the boulder for support, she tried her best to stand.

"Stay there, don't move, and keep your head down. We'll deal with the moonstruck." A naked woman had stepped out from behind the boulder! She was tall — almost six feet - and had either brown or red hair — it was difficult to tell in the moonlight. She was joined a moment later by two massive shapes. As big as the creature that had attacked her, but these wolves walked on four legs instead of two. Then, the woman dropped into a crouch and began to change. Her body shifted, stretched, and reformed. Bones seemed to shatter with a sickening crunch — realigning themselves into a different form. Thick hair sprouted from her pores, flowing across the woman's back and arms while her mouth elongated, razor-sharp fangs bursting through her gums. All of this only took a matter of seconds, but it seemed to take forever for Connie. She backed against the boulder, hand over her mouth in abject horror. Not only were these monsters real, but instead of one, she was now faced with four of them.

The three quadruped werewolves turned and sprinted up the slope to the bipedal creature that was still struggling to extract the jagged wooden spike from its back. It registered the three new werewolves, snarled a challenge, and then hurled itself down the mountainside to meet their assault. The bipedal creature that had attacked her was fast and utterly lethal. Still, it seemed to be operating on little more than rage and instinct. It slashed out at its assailants while the other wolves feigned attacks, then changed direction when the biped committed, opening itself up to an attack from one of the others. Teeth and claws raked the beast, opening terrible wounds before they danced back out of range once more. As the monster turned to attack one wolf, another inflicted horrific damage to it from behind. Soon, the mountainside was slick with black ichor, its coppery stink reaching Connie where she hid, making her sick to her stomach. The dance did not last long. With each attack, the monstrous bipedal werewolf became weaker; its counter-attacks became less focused and slower. After only a few minutes, it fell to one knee. That was when the wolf that had been the brown-haired woman surged forward, clamped her jaws around its throat, and squeezed. The beast cried out in agony – a strangled, bubbling cry of pain that was abruptly cut off as the female werewolf's jaws clamped shut, severing its head in a single bite. The head rolled down the mountainside, coming to rest beside Connie's hiding place.

She looked down instinctively and let out a cry of alarm and grief. She was looking at the severed head of Steve, her boyfriend. Connie felt numb, unable to understand how or why this had happened. Her emotions were too raw, even for tears to come. A shadow fell over her, blocking out the moonlight. "Knew him, did you? We've been tracking him for a couple of months now. Poor bastard probably didn't even know he was infected. He got clipped in Germany a while back when we took down another rogue – he probably thought he'd been nipped by a stray dog and got a rabies shot."

It all made sense. Steve had told her about getting bitten by a dog a few months ago. He'd not gone into detail, though – he knew that despite her love of horror movies, she couldn't stand even the mention of any real-life injuries. She thought about the slashes on her back and let out a sob. Was she destined to become the same? A ravenous monster that killed everything it came into contact with every full moon?

The brown-haired woman frowned. "The bastard got you good, I'm afraid. I think you'd better come with us."

Connie looked at the severed head of her boyfriend. She couldn't go back to her old life. Not now. Not like this. Couldn't risk hurting her family or friends. There was no way she could know what would happen to her, but if they were going to kill her, they could have done it easily where she lay. They may even be able to help. She bit back her tears, then reached out and took the woman's hand. "Yes, ah suppose ah really should."

The End

Rug
By
Graham Masterton

Masterton is the son of an Army officer, and the setting of "Rug" will be familiar to all those one-time children of BAOR who were schooled in England and visited their parents in Germany in the holidays. As the author reveals: "The real wolfskin rug hung in a shop filled with antique bric-a-brac in Munster, Westphalia. The house and the horse are real. Only the family have been changed to protect those who are frightened by claws scratching at the window...

Two days later, and nearly 75 kilometres away, a tall woman entered an antique shop close to the thirteenth-century Buddensturm, in the cathedral town of Münster. The doorbell jangled on a spring; the morning sunlight illuminated antlers and stags' heads and display cases of stuffed foxes.

The shop owner appeared from behind a curtain, smoking a cigarette. The woman was standing against the light, so that it was difficult for him to see her face.

"*Ich möchte eine Relsedecke,*" she said. "*Eine Relsedecke, gnädige Frau?*"

"*Ja. Ich möchte ein Wolfshaut.*"

"*Ein Wolfshaut? Das ist rar.* Very difficult to find, you understand?"

"Yes, I understand. But you can find me one, yes?" "*Ich weiss nicht.* I can try."

The woman took out a small black purse, unfastened the clasp, and gave the shop owner 1,000DM, neatly folded. "Deposit," she said. "*Depositum.* If you can find me a wolfskin rug, I will pay you more. Much more."

She wrote a telephone number on the back of one of his cards, blew it dry and gave it to him.

"Don't fail me," she said.

But when she had left the shop (the doorbell still ringing) the shop owner stood still for a very long time. Then he opened one of the drawers underneath his counter and took out a dark, tarnished nail. A steel nail, heavily plated with silver.

They didn't come looking for wolfskins very often, but when they did, they were usually desperate, which made them even more vulnerable than ever. Still, he needed practice. He needed to tease her along. He needed to build up her hopes. He needed to make her believe that here, at last, was a man that she could trust.

Then it would be tree time. The hammer and the heart.

The woman didn't look back at the shop as she left it. Even if she *had* done, she may not have understood the significance of its name. After all, one beast simply passed on his ferocity to the next; not caring about names or heritage or marital vows. The only thing that was important was the skin, the *Wolfshaut*, the hairy covering that gave everything meaning.

But the name of the shop was "Bremke: Jagerkunst," and its business was not only the art and artefacts of hunting, but the relentless pursuit of the hunters themselves.

John found the wolf on the third day, when everybody else had gone to Paderborn for the horse trials. He had pleaded an earache (earaches were always best because nobody could prove whether you really had one or not, and you were still allowed to read and listen to the radio.) The truth was, though, that he was already homesick, and he didn't feel like doing anything but sitting by himself and thinking miserably about mummy.

The Smythe-Barnetts were very kind to him. Mrs Smythe-Barnett always kissed him goodnight, and their two daughters Penny and Veronica tried their best to involve him in everything they did. But the truth was that he was too sad to be much fun, and he shunned affection because it made a terrible prickly lump rise up in his throat, like a sea-urchin, and his eyes fill with tears.

He stood in the bay window in the front of the house watching the Smythe-Barnetts drive away with their smartly varnished horsebox in tow. The exhaust from Col. Smythe-Barnett's Land Rover drifted away between the scabby plane trees, and the street fell silent again. It was one of those colourless autumn mornings when he could easily believe that he would never see blue sky again, ever. From Aachen to the Teutoburger Wald, the north German plains were suffocating under a comforter of greyish-white cloud.

In the kitchen, John could hear the German maid singing as she mopped the beige-tiled floor, "Wooden Heart" in German. Everybody was singing it because Elvis had just released *GI Blues*.

He knew that everything would be better next week. His father had ten days' leave, and they were going to take a Rhine steamer to Koblenz, and then they were going to spend a week at the Forces recreation centre at Winterberg, among the pine forests of the Sauerland. But that still couldn't ease the homesickness of staying with a strange family in a strange country, with his parents so recently divorced. His grandmother had said something about "all those long separations ... a man's only human, you know." John wasn't at all sure what she meant by "only human". It sounded to him like only *just* human – as if beneath those pond green cardigans and those tattersall-check shirts there throbbed the heart of a creature far more primitive. He had even heard mummy saying about his father "he can be a beast at times", and he thought of his father arching back his head and baring his teeth, his eyes filled up with scarlet and his hands crooked like claws.

He went into the kitchen, but the floor was still wet and the maid shooed him away. She was a big-faced woman in black, and she smelled of cabbagey sweat. It seemed to John that all Germans smelled of cabbagey sweat. Penny had taken him on the bus to Bielefeld yesterday afternoon, and the smell of cabbagey sweat had been overwhelming.

He went out into the garden. The lawns were studded with fallen apples. He kicked one of them so that it hit the side of the stable. John had already been told off for trying to feed the Smythe-Barnetts' horse with apples. "They give him gripes, you stupid boy," Veronica had snapped at him. How was *he* supposed to know? The only horse he had ever seen at close-quarters was the milkman's horse from United Dairies, and that wore a permanent nosebag.

He sat on the swing and creaked backward and forward for a while. The garden was almost unbearably silent. Still, this was better than being introduced to all of the Smythe- Barnett's haw-hawing friends in

Paderborn. He had seen them packing their picnic lunch and it was salami and fatty beef sandwiches.

He looked up at the huge suburban house. It was typical of large family residences built in Germany between the wars, with an orange-tiled roof and fawn concrete-rendered walls. There must have been another similar house next door, but Bielefeld had been badly bombed, and now there was nothing left but a wild orchard and brick foundations.

John heard a harsh croaking noise. He looked up and saw a stork perched on the chimney – a real-live stork. It was the first one he had ever seen, and he could hardly believe it was real. It was like an omen, a warning of things to come. It stayed on the chimney for only a few moments, turning its beak imperiously from right to left, its feathers ruffled. Then it flew away, with an audible *flap, flap, flap* of its wings.

While he was looking up, John noticed for the first time that there was a dormer window in the roof: only a small one. There must be an attic or another bedroom right at the top of the house. If there was an attic, there might be something interesting in it, like relics from the war, or an unexploded bomb, or books about sex. He had found a book about sex in the attic at home, *Everything Newlyweds Should Know*. He had traced Fig. 6 – The Female Vulva and coloured it pink.

He went back inside the house. The maid was in the living-room now, polishing the furniture and filling the air with the aroma of lavender and cabbagey sweat. John climbed the stairs to the first landing, where the walls were hung with photographs of Penny and Veronica on Jupiter, each photograph decorated with a red rosette. He was glad he hadn't gone with them to Paderborn. Why should he care if their stupid horse managed to jump over a whole lot of poles?

He climbed the second flight of stairs. He hadn't been up here before. This was where Col. and Mrs Smythe-Barnett had their "sweet." John didn't know why they felt it necessary to eat their pudding in their bedroom. He supposed it was just another of those things that snobby people like the Smythe-Barnetts always did, like having silver napkin-rings and serving tomato ketchup in a dish.

The floorboards creaked. Through the half-open doors, John could see the corner of the Smythe-Barnetts' bed, and Mrs Smythe-Barnett's dressing-table, with its array of silver backed brushes. He listened for a moment. Downstairs, the maid had started to vacuum-clean the living-room carpet. Her cleaner made a roaring drone like a German bomber. She wouldn't be able to hear him at all.

Cautiously, he crept into the Smythe-Barnetts' bedroom, and across to the dressing-table. In the mirror, he could see a solemn, white-faced boy of 11 with a short prickly haircut and sticky-out ears. This of course was not him but simply his external disguise, the physical manifestation he adopted in order to put up his hand during school register and say "Present, miss!"

On the dressing-table lay a half-finished letter on blue deckle-edged notepaper, with a fountain pen lying across it. It read "very disturbed and withdrawn, but I suppose that's only natural under the circumstances. He cries himself to sleep every night, and suffers nightmares. He also seems to find it very difficult to get along with other children. It will obviously take a great deal of time and..."

He stared at his pasty face in the mirror. He looked like a photograph of his father when his father was very young. *Very disturbed and withdrawn.* How could Mrs Smythe-Barnett have written that about him? He wasn't disturbed and withdrawn. It was just that what was inside him, he wanted to *keep* inside. Why should he let Mrs Smythe-Barnett know how unhappy he was? What did it have to do with *her*?

He tiptoed out of the Smythe-Barnetts' bedroom and quietly closed the door. The German maid was still leading a full-scale raid over London Docks. He walked along to the end of the corridor, and it was there that he discovered a small cream- painted door which obviously led up to the attic. He opened it. Inside, there was a steep flight of hessian-carpeted stairs. It was very gloomy up there, although a little of the grey, muted daylight managed to penetrate. John could smell mustiness, and dust, and an odd odour like onion flowers.

He climbed the stairs. As he did so, he came face to face with the wolf.

It was lying flat on the floor, facing him. Its eyes were yellow, and its teeth were bared, and its dry, purplish tongue was hanging out. Its hairy ears were slightly motheaten, and there was a baldish patch on the side of its snout, but that did nothing to detract from its ferocity. Even if its body was utterly empty, and it was now being used as a rug, it was still a wolf, and a huge wolf at that — the biggest wolf that John had ever seen.

He looked around the attic. Apart from a partitioned-off area at the far end, to house the water-tanks, it had been converted into a spare bedroom which ran the whole length and breadth of the house. Behind the wolf there was a solid brass bed, with a sagging mattress on it. Three ill-assorted armchairs were arranged by the window, and an old, varnished chest-of-drawers stood beneath the lowest part of the eaves.

There was a framed photograph hanging by the side of the dormer window. The top of the frame was decorated with dried flowers, long ago leached of any colour. The photograph showed a fair-haired girl standing by the side of a suburban road somewhere, one eye closed against the sunlight. She was wearing an embroidered halter-top dress and a white blouse.

John knelt down beside the wolf-rug and examined it closely. He reached out and touched the tips of its curving teeth. It was incredible to think this had once been a real animal, running through the woods, chasing after hares and deer, maybe even people.

He stroked its fur. It was still wiry and thick, mostly black, with some grey streaks around the throat. He wondered who had shot it, and why. If *he* had a wolf, he wouldn't shoot it. He would train it to hunt people down, and tear their throats out. Particularly his maths teacher, Mrs Bennett. She would look good with her throat turned out. Blood creeping across the pages of *School Mathematics Part One by H.E. Parr*.

He buried his nose in the wolf-rug's flanks and breathed in, to find out if it still smelled at all like an animal. All he could detect, however, was dust, and a very faint leathery odour. Whatever wolf-scent this beast had ever possessed, it had dried up with age.

For an hour or two, until it was lunchtime, he played hunters. Then he played Tarzan, and wrestled with the wolf-rug all over the bedroom. He clamped its jaws around his wrist, and grunted and heaved in an effort to prevent it from biting off his hand. Finally, he managed to get it onto its back, and he stabbed it again and again with his huge imaginary jungle-knife, ripping out its guts, and twisting the blade deep into its heart.

A few minutes after twelve, he heard the maid calling him. He straightened the rug, and hurried quickly and quietly downstairs. The maid was ready to leave, in a hat and coat and gloves, all black. On the kitchen table there was a plateful of cold salami and gherkins and buttered bread, and a large glass of warm milk, on the surface of which the yellow cream had already begun to form into blobby clusters.

That night, after the Smythe-Barnetts returned, all tired and noisy and smelling of horses and sherry, John lay in his small bed staring at the ceiling and thinking of the wolf. It was so proud, so fierce, and yet so dead, lying gutted on the attic floor with its eyes staring at nothing at all. It had been a beast at times, just like his father; and perhaps one day it could be a beast again. There was no telling with creatures like that, as his grandmother had once said, with her hand cupped over the telephone receiver, as if he wouldn't be able to hear.

The wind was getting up and clearing away the cloud; but at the same time, it was making the plane tree branches dip and thrash, so that strange spiky shadows shuddered and danced across the ceiling of John's bedroom, shadows like praying- mantises, and spider-legs, and wolf-claws.

In the eye of the coming gale, he closed his eyes and tried to sleep. But the spider-legs danced even more frantically on the ceiling, and the praying-mantises dipped and shivered, and every quarter-hour the Smythe-Barnetts' hall clock struck the Westminster chimes, as if to remind themselves all through the night how correct they were, both in timing and in taste.

And then at quarter past two in the morning he heard a scratching sound coming down the attic stairs. He was sure of it. The wolf! The wolf was climbing down the attic stairs with arched back and bristled tail, its eyes gleaming amber as garnets in the darkness, its breath panting *hah-hah-HAH-hah! hah-hah- HAH-hah*! Ripe with wolfishness and bloodlust.

He heard it running along the corridor, past the Smythe-Barnetts' sweet, hungry, hungry, hungry. He heard it sniffing at door locks, growling in its throat. He heard it pause at the head of the second-floor staircase, and then plunge downwards, coming his way.

It began to run really fast now, its tail beating against the walls of the corridor. Its eyes opened wide and yellow, and its ears stiffened up. It was coming after him, coming to take its revenge. He shouldn't have fought it, shouldn't have wrestled it, and for all that his jungle-knife was imaginary, he had still intended to cut its heart out, he had still *wanted* to do it, even if he hadn't.

He heard the wolf thudding toward his bedroom door, louder and louder, and then the door burst open and John shot up in bed and screamed and screamed, his eyes tight shut, his fists clenched, wetting his pyjamas in sheer terror.

Mrs Smythe-Barnett came into the room and took him in her arms. She switched on his bedside lamp and cuddled him and shushed him. He put up with her cuddling for two or three minutes and then he had to pull away. His wet pyjama trousers were rapidly chilling, and he felt so embarrassed that he could have happily died at that moment. Yet he had no alternative but to stand shivering in a dressing-gown while she patiently changed the bed for him, and brought him clean pyjamas, and tucked him up. A tall, big-nosed woman in a tall nightdress, wearing a scarf to cover the rollers in her hair. Saintly, in a way, but a Bernini saint; marble-perfect, always able to cope. He so much missed his mummy, who couldn't cope with anything, or not very well.

"You had a nightmare," said Mrs Smythe-Barnett, stroking his forehead.

"It's all right. I'm all right now," John told her, almost crossly. "How's your earache?" she asked him.

"Better, thanks. I saw a stork."

"That's nice. Actually, storks are quite common around here; but the local people think they're bad luck. They say that if a stork perches on your roof, somebody in the house will get the very worst thing they ever feared. I think that's why they say that storks bring babies! But I don't believe in superstitions like that, do you?"

John shook his head. He couldn't understand where the wolf had gone. The wolf had come running down the stairs and along the corridor and down the second flight of stairs and along the corridor and—

And here was Mrs Smythe-Barnett, stroking his forehead.

He took the bus into Bielefeld the next day, on his own this time. He suffered the cabbagey sweat and the Ernte 23 cigarettes, squashed between a huge woman dressed in black and a thin youth with a long hair growing out of the mole on his chin.

He went to the cake-shop and bought an apfelstrudel with piles of squirty cream on it, which he ate as he walked along the street. When he saw his reflection in shop windows, he couldn't believe how young he was. He went into a bookshop and looked through some illustrated art books. Some of them had pictures of nudes. He found an etching by Hans Bellmer of a pregnant woman being penetrated by two men at once, her baby crowded to one side of her womb by two thrusting penises. Her head was thrown back to swallow the penis of a third man, faceless, anonymous.

He was about to leave the bookshop when he saw an etching on the wall of a wolf. On closer inspection, however, it wasn't a wolf at all, but a man with the face of a wolf. The caption, in black Gothic lettering, read Wolfmensch. John went up and peered at it more closely. The man-wolf was standing in front of an old German town, with crowded rooftops. On one of those rooftops perched a stork.

He was still staring at the picture when the bookshop proprietor approached him – a small, balding, thin-cheeked man with yellowish skin and a worn-out grey suit, and breath that was thick with tobacco.

"You're English?" he asked. John nodded.

"You're interested in wolf-men?"

"I don't know. Not specially."

"Well, anyway, this picture in which you show so much interest, he is our famous local wolf-man, from Bielefeld. His real name was Schmidt, Gunther Schmidt. He lived – you see the dates here – from 1887 to 1923. He was the son of a schoolmaster."

"Did he ever kill anybody?" asked John.

"Yes, they say so," nodded the bookshop proprietor. "They say he killed many young women, when they were out walking in the woods."

John said nothing, but stared at the wolf-man in awe. The wolf-man looked so much like the rug in the

Smythe-Barnetts' attic – eyes and fangs and hairy ears – but then he supposed that all wolves looked much the same. Met one wolf-man, met them all.

The bookshop proprietor hooked the picture down from the wall. "Nobody knows how Gunther Schmidt became a wolf- man. Some people say that his ancestor was bitten by a wolf-man mercenary during the Thirty Years' War. There's a legend, you see, that when the Diet of Ratisbon called back General Wallenstein, he brought in some very strange mercenaries to help him. He was beaten by Gustavus at the battle of Lützen, but many of Gustavus' men had terrible wounds, throats torn open, and suchlike. Well, perhaps it isn't true. But it's true that the battle of Lützen was fought under a full moon, and you know what they say about wolf-people. Women, as well as men."

"Werewolves," said John, feeling awed.

"That's right, werewolves! Here, let me show you this book. It has pictures of all of the incidents of werewolves, during the past fifty years. It's a very interesting book, if you like to be scared!"

From the shelf just above his desk, he took down a large album, covered with brown paper. He opened it out, and beckoned John to take a look.

"Here! This is one for the werewolf enthusiast! Lili Bauer, killed on the night of April 20, 1921, in

Tecklenburg, her throat was torn open. And here is Mara Thiele, found dead in the Lippe, July 19, 1921, also throat torn open ... *und so weiter, und so weiter.*"

"Who's this?" asked John. He had found a photograph of a girl in a halter-top dress, with a white blouse, and blonde hair, standing by a suburban road, one eye squinched against the sunlight.

"This one ... Lotte Bremke, found dead in the woods close to Heepen, August 15, 1923. Again, throat ripped out. The last victim, this is what it says. After that, nobody heard from Gunther Schmidt anything more ... although here, look. A human heart was found nailed to a tree in Waldstrasse, with the message, here is the heart of the wolf."

John stared at the photograph of Lotte Bremke for a long time. He was sure that it was the same girl whose photograph was nailed up in the attic at the Smythe-Barnetts' house. But could that mean that Lotte Bremke had lived there once? And if she had — where had the wolf-skin come from? Had Lotte Bremke's father killed the wolf-man, perhaps, and nailed his heart to a tree, and kept his skin as a gruesome souvenir?

He closed the book and handed it back. The bookshop proprietor was watching him with pale, disinterested eyes, their pupils the colour of cold tea.

"Well?" said the bookshop proprietor. "*Wass glaubst du?*" "I'm not really interested in werewolves," John told him.

There were far worse things than werewolves, like wetting the bed in front of Mrs Smythe-Barnett.

"But you stared at this picture," the bookshop proprietor smiled.

"I was just interested."

"Well ... of course. But don't forget that the beast is not inside us. This is important to remember when dealing with wolf-men. The beast is not inside us. *We are inside the beast, versteh?*"

John stared at him. He didn't know what to say. He felt as if this man could read everything that he was thinking, like an open book lying on a shallow riverbed. All that was required to turn the pages was to get one's fingers wet.

John took the bus back to Heepen. It was nearly half-past five and the sky was indigo. The moon hung over the Teutoburger Wald like the bright face of God. When he arrived back at the Smythe-Barnett's house, all the lights were lit, Penny and Veronica were giggling in the kitchen, and Col. Smythe-Barnett was entertaining six or seven fellow-officers in the living-room (roars of laughter, clouds of cigarette-smoke).

Mrs Smythe-Barnett came into the kitchen and for the first time John was pleased to see her. She was wearing a glittery cocktail-dress, but her face was dark with rage. "Where have you been?" she shouted, and she was so angry that it took him a moment or two to understand that she was shouting at him.

"I went to Bielefeld," he said, weakly.

"You went to Bielefeld without telling us! We've been frantic! Gerald had to call the local polizei, for God's sake, and you don't have any idea how much he hates asking for help from the locals!"

"I'm sorry," he said. "I thought it was all right. We went on Tuesday. I thought it was all right to go today."

"For God's sake, isn't it enough that we're wet nursing you? You've only been here four days and you've been nothing but trouble! No wonder your parents broke up!"

John sat with his head bowed and said nothing. He didn't understand adult drunkenness. He didn't understand that people could exaggerate things that irritated them, and not really mean it, and say sorry the next morning, and it was all forgotten. He was eleven.

Veronica set his supper in front of him. It was a cold chicken leg, with gherkins. He had asked especially not to be given warm milk, because he didn't like it. Instead, Veronica had poured him a glass of flat Coca-Cola.

In bed that night, he crunched himself up and cried as if his heart would split into pieces.

But at two o'clock in the morning, he opened his eyes, and he was perfectly calm. The moon was shining so brightly through his bedroom curtains that it could have been daylight. Dead daylight, the world of the dead, but daylight all the same.

He climbed out of bed and looked at himself in his little mirror. A boy with a face made of silver. He said, "Lotte Bremke". That was all he had to say. He knew that she had lived here, when the house was first built. He knew what had happened to her. Some things are so obvious to children that they blink in disbelief when adults fail to understand. Lotte Bremke's father had done what any father would do, and hunted down the wolf-man, and killed him, somehow, and nailed his heart (*smash*! quiver! *smash*! quiver) to the nearest plane tree.

John glided to the bedroom door, and opened it. He walked along the corridor with feet like glass. He walked up the stairs, and along the second corridor, with feet like glass. He opened the cream-painted door that led to the attic, and opened it.

He climbed the stairs. Sure enough, the wolf-rug was waiting for him, with gleaming yellow eyes and bristly fur. John crawled across the rough hessian carpet on hands and knees and stroked it, and whispered, "Wolfman, that's what you were. Don't deny it. You were on the outside, weren't you? You were the skin. That was the difference; that was what nobody understood. Werewolves are wolves turned into men, not men turned into wolves! And you ran round their houses, didn't you, and ran through their woods, and caught them, and bit them, and tore their throats out, and killed them!"

"But they caught you, didn't they, wolf, and they took out the man who was hiding inside you. They took out all of your insides, and left you with nothing but your skin.

"Still, you shouldn't worry. I can be your man now. I can put you on. You can be a rug one minute, and a real wolf the next." He stood up, and lifted the rug up from the floor. It had felt heavy when he had been wrestling with it this afternoon, but now it felt even heavier, almost as heavy as a live wolf. It took him all of his strength to lift it around his shoulders, and to drape the empty legs around him. He perched the head on top of his own head.

He trailed around the attic, around and around. "I am the wolf, and the wolf is me," he breathed to himself. "I am the wolf, and the wolf is me."

He closed his eyes. He flared his nostrils. I'm a wolf now, he thought to himself. Fierce and fast and dangerous. He could imagine himself running through the woods of Heepen, in between the trees, his paws padding soft and deadly over the thick carpet of pine-needles.

He opened his eyes. Now was the time to get his revenge. The wolf's revenge! He climbed down the stairs with his tail beating thump, thump, thump on the treads behind him. He pushed open the attic door and began to lope along the corridor, toward the slightly-open door of the Smythe-Barnetts' bedroom.

He growled deep down in his throat, and saliva began to drip from the sides of his mouth. He made hardly any sound at all as he approached the Smythe-Barnetts' door.

I am the wolf, and the wolf is me.

He was only three or four feet away from the door when it suddenly and silently opened, and the corridor was filled with moonlight.

John hesitated for a moment, and growled again.

Then something stepped out of the Smythe-Barnetts' bedroom that made the real hair rise on the back of his neck, and turned his soul to water.

It was Mrs Smythe-Barnett, and yet it wasn't. She was naked, tall and naked – but she was more than naked, she was *raw*. Her body glistened with white bone and tightly stretched membranes, and John could even see her arteries pulsing, and the fanlike tracery of her veins.

Inside her long, narrow ribcage, her lungs rose and fell in a quick, obscene panting.

Her face was horrifying. It seemed to have stretched out into a long bony snout, and her lips were drawn tightly back over her teeth. Her eyes glittered yellow. Wolf-yellow.

"*Where's my skin?*" she demanded, in a voice that was halfway between a hiss and a growl. "*What are you doing with my skin?*"

John let the wolf-rug drop from his shoulders and slide down onto the floor. He couldn't speak. He couldn't even breathe. He watched in helpless dread as Mrs Smythe-Barnett dropped down onto her hands and knees, and seemed to slither into the wolf-rug like a naked hand slithering into a furry glove.

"I didn't *mean* to—" he managed to choke out, but then the claws burst into his windpipe, knocking him backward against the wall. He swallowed, so that he could scream, but all that he swallowed was a half-pint of warm blood.

The wolf-rug came after him and there was nothing that he could do to stop it.

John's father arrived at the house shortly after eight-thirty the following morning, so that he could see John for five or ten minutes before he went to work. His German driver kept the engine of the khaki Volkswagen running, because it was so cold this morning, well below five degrees.

He went up the steps, his swagger-stick tucked under his arm. To his surprise, the front door was wide open. He pressed the doorbell, and then stepped inside the house.

"David? Helen? Anyone at home?"

He heard a strange mewing noise coming from the kitchen. "Helen? Is everything all right?"

He walked through to the back of the house. In the kitchen he found the German maid sitting at the table, still dressed in her hat and coat, her handbag in front of her, shaking and shivering with shock.

"What's wrong?" John's father demanded. "Where is everybody?"

"*Etwas shrecklich*." the maid quivered. "All family dead."

"What? What do you mean, 'all family dead'?"

"Upstairs," said the maid. "All family dead."

"Call my driver. Tell him to come inside. Then telephone the police. *Polizei*, got it?"

Filled with terrible apprehension, John's father climbed the stairs. On the first-floor landing, he found the bedroom doors ajar, and spattered with blood. The smiling photographs of Penny and Veronica lay smashed on the carpet, the red gymkhana rosettes trampled and torn. He went close to the girls' bedroom doors and looked inside. Penny lay sprawled on her back, her neck so furiously ripped open that her head was almost separated from her body. Veronica lay facedown, her white nightgown stained dark red. Grim-faced, John's father went to the bedroom where John was sleeping. He opened the door, but inside the bed was empty, and there was no sign of John. He swallowed dryly, and said a prayer to himself. Please God, let him still be alive.

He climbed further. The second-story corridor was sprayed with squiggles and question-marks of blood. In the Smythe- Barnetts' bedroom, Col. Smythe-Barnett lay on his back staring at the ceiling, his larynx torn out. He looked as if he were wearing a bib of blood. No sign of Helen Smythe-Barnett anywhere.

The door that led to the staircase was decorated all over with bloody hand marks. John's father opened it, took a deep breath, and slowly climbed up to the attic.

The room was filled with sunlight. As he entered, he found himself confronted by a rug made of wolfskin, with the wolf's head still attached. The wolf's jaws were dark with congealing blood, and its fur was matted.

There was something concealed by the rug that raised it in a slight hump. John's father hesitated for a very long time, and then took hold of the edge of the rug and lifted it up.

Underneath it was the half-digested remains of a young boy.

The End

"Harry's Inevitable Extinction"
By
Glenn Rolfe

"Are you nuts?"

Eddie dropped his cigar to the ground and crushed it beneath his alligator skin boot. "You want the job or not?"

Harry Pearson didn't want *this* job—he was a private dick, not animal control or a Van Helsing—, but the rent wasn't turning tricks or running a hot dog cart. "Yeah, fuck it. I'll start tonight, but I want half up front."

Eddie Cosby, a filthy rich East Texan by way of Shreveport, Louisiana and his Hilcorp oil company, pulled a thick clip of bills from inside his white dress coat, licked his sausage thumb, counted out several twenties and fifties, and tucked the money into the chest pocket of Harry's checked shirt. "Two things," Eddie said. "One, you get $500 to start."

Harry didn't bother checking the cash. Cosby was always good for it. He took his Stetson hat off and dusted it off against his jeans, ran a hand through his medium length hair and put the hat back in place. "What's the other?"

The big man turned to toward the high noon sun before glancing back at Harry. "You better start now, while it's still daylight."

Harry walked to his Rambler and opened the door. "You really buying into this monster angle? Doesn't seem like you."

"Well, Harry, you take a look over the photos in that file sitting in your apartment and you might start thinking about what's possible in the world and what ain't." Eddie Cosby climbed behind the seat of his Cadillac. "You'll come to see why this one has got me locking all my doors at night. See ya, Harry. Call me if you find...anything."

Harry watched the Caddy pull away through the cloud of dry Texas dust.

He spat and sunk into the Rambler's seat, turned the key in the ignition and cranked the am/fm stereo. ZZ Top's "La Grange" thumped its way through his veins, He dropped the car into Drive and tore off down the blacktop thinking about fangs, hairy beasts, and horror movies.

The witness statements were insane; the photos were goddamn terrifying.

The bodies were mangled. He'd never seen actual photos of people that had been eaten by animals. Victim after victim with their chest cavities hollowed out, appendages ravaged, and ligaments and bones that were never meant to be seen outside of an OR table or X-ray image on full display in each photo. Eddie's lack of faith in the police finding out the truth behind these deaths made sense.

Eddie's daughter's photo was not included in the file, but the info in the coroner's report in Eddie had obtained painted the gruesome picture just fine.

Nina Cosby was reported missing last month. Two weeks ago, the remains were discovered behind the Antler Transfer station off Highway 80. Like the other poor souls, her chest had been gnawed into, left hand bitten off, claw marks slashing her once pretty face into ribbons. On top of all that, she'd been violated. *Not* your average animal attack.

The microwave clock read: 2:27. Time was a wasting.

Harry tossed his hair back and grabbed his hat.

He pulled the Rambler up to the paint chipped transfer station gate.

Open Monday, Wednesday, Saturday. 7-5pm
Fucking Fridays.

A cheap padlock held the two waist high gates together. Harry grabbed the little sledge from his backseat and broke the lock with one swing.

He hoped no one was there as he drove along past each recycling station, followed by the four trash compactors.

A road wound around the building marked: Large furniture. He followed it and saw an awe-inspiring oak forest as its backdrop. Something so magically beautiful behind a business of trash and used plastics seemed almost wrong.

Harry parked, killed the engine and stepped out into the day.

Nina's body was found by a worker taking a piss just a little ways into the woods. Harry lit a cigarette and walked to the long-branched trees. He hadn't grown up in East Texas. New England had nothing close to this. Stopping just shy of the first impressive tree, a child before a fantastic new land, Harry wondered about the beast responsible for Nina's brutal demise.

There were black bears in this part of the state, but they landed on the protection list. It was the rape that put a bullet in the skull of that theory. Unless she was assaulted just prior to the animal attack, but that's not what the report said.

His watch read: 3:36.

That gave him just over three hours before nightfall.

Eddie's wolfman howled in the back of Harry's mind.

Bullshit or otherwise, gorgeous forest or not, Harry's gut told him not to be here alone longer than needed.

He took the last drag off his smoke and put the butt out on the bottom of his boot. They got more rain in this part of Texas, but it had been dryer than usual the last few weeks. He wasn't taking any chances.

Stepping over the imaginary threshold, Harry tried to shake off the ghastly feeling clinging to his spine and started toward the kill zone.

It was only thirty feet in, but that short distance was far enough to make the transfer station suddenly feel like the space shuttle and the woods to be the void of space.

A branch snapped, cracking like a gunshot in the silence.

Harry closed his eyes and held his breath.

His heart throttled the inside of his chest. A cold sweat broke to life over his skin. Visions from the series of murder scene photos he committed to memory flashed like an end-of-life reel upon the canvas behind his closed eyelids.

Inhaling deep, Harry opened his eyes and found solitude was still his only partner in this case.

Eddie, remind me to throat punch you for this.

There was a heart carved into the Oak tree with the initials GR – SM. They could be anyone in the world, Gretta Rodriguez and Seth Meyer for all Harry gave a shit, but it meant he was in the right place.

This was where they found Nina.

The blood was gone, as were the bits and pieces of her remains, but the tree was there. Her ghost was here. Harry might have a hard time buying werewolves, vampires, and chupa-fucking-cabras, but ever since Grammy Evylin, he most goddamn assuredly believed in ghosts.

Evie, as Granpa Vinnie referred to her, talked with the dead. And not for money like some capitalist snake oil sales-bitch. Evie brought families back together and talked poltergeists into retirement. Evie Pearson was the real deal. When Harry and his brother Chris were 12 and 14 respectively, Grammy Evylin let them speak to their dead sister Carolyn. Carolyn passed from a rare heart condition when she was only seven. She was two years older than Chris, at the time. But both Harry and Chris were extremely close with their big sis. And in the summer of '81, they missed her like crazy. Grammy Evylin brought the boys into her basement where she held her seances. Holding hands in the dark, whispering prayers to conjure her spirit, Harry and Chris were not surprised when their big sis began to speak to them.

Another gunshot branch cracked and broke Harry free of his reverie.

He spun around to see a man with a large unibrow and two mean ugly eyes looking down at him. A mountain of a human. That was his last thought before the bastard clobbered him over the head.

Rain drops pattered his cheeks, waking Harry from his slumber.

A bruised sky, cloudy with the chance of death, swallowed what remained of the late September afternoon. He was alive, but he was effectively tied to an oak tree.

Harry brought his hazy gaze to the large man pacing before him. "You shouldn't have come here, friend."

"You—" Harry said.

"Shut your fucking mouth," the man roared, as he launched toward Harry, stopping inches from his face.

The scent of spoiled meat came to life between them. Harry bit back the urge to vomit.

The man was dressed in dirt-stained sweats and a ragged Nickelback tee. His bare feet were dark with soil and dust, and he was sporting a wonky ass, patchy beard. The big bastard had to be living in the woods.

"You shut up, or I'll..." the stranger was suddenly distant, his eyes lost, drifting in the vastness of space.

"Listen, man," Harry said. "I was paid to check out this scene and give an assessment. That's all. I don't know you from nothing and I just want to collect my paycheck and move the hell on."

The behemoth rose, turned his wide back and began to laugh.

Harry's faith in everything—God, Karma, the Dallas Cowboys—all went out the window. This was Nina Cosby's killer.

And Harry was in a bad fucking place.

"What are you?" Harry asked.

"What are any of us?"

Whatever the hell that was supposed to mean.

Harry waited.

"Why does a lonely young man buy an assault rifle, enter a school of children and unleash hell? What happens to a mother in the grip of opioids that overrides her code and allows her to neglect her infant? Are we not all just as capable of evil as we are good? Is it a choice or destiny?"

This guy wasn't totally disconnected from society, but he was standing in the exit line. Harry's initial thoughts were that he might talk his way out of this situation. That locomotive had gone off the rails like

Ozzy's crazy train. This was going to play out in one of two ways. He was going to fight his way out and run or he would die.

Around them, the graying daylight clinging to life gave in to the night.

"This is the animal kingdom. It's not a place for the meek, though sometimes they do find ways to hang on, to co-exist through anxiety riddled days praying to false deities that this won't be the day get swallowed into extinction. But is that really living?"

"What's your name?" Harry stalled, trying to flex his muscles testing his bindings. The ropes were tight. He wasn't getting free unless this monster got overconfident and decided to play games.

The man waved him off. "Names are important, but not here." A tremor seemed to run through the man's arm. When he spoke again, it was as if he had to work hard to form the words. "Not now." He turned.

And Harry saw his eyes and felt something inside trying to shrink.

This was the killer, and he was more than a man.

"Not for what I am."

The transformation took place much faster than what Harry could remember from any movie. The one in London, the one in the Jackson kid's video. The man was there one minute and gone the next. In his place, something ancient, something impossible, something lethal.

"I... I ...don't want to die here. Not like this."

He thought the man had been intimidating before...this abomination grew in every way. It was like the Incredible Hulk but bigger and harrier.

And worst of all, *real*.

The wolfman let out a snort and a snarl that resonated far beyond them. The low, guttural growl like Satan's Harley just rumbling in place, waiting to open up and let you know what it could really do caused Harry to piss himself.

And the monster lowered itself to the earth, the arms of the Oaks surrounding it, like the arms of ancient magical priests praying for the Armageddon that was sure to follow, its snout raised, sniffing out his fear.

On all fours, the creature stalked toward him. The limited light from the moon buried behind the clouds gave away only the beast's shape. Harry could hardly make out many details but did catch a reflection form those ugly yellowed eyes as the monster stopped.

It's taking pleasure in this moment.

This wasn't worth five hundred dollars.

Harry shut his eyes, and through shaky breaths began to cry.

The howl Harry anticipated never came. Instead, the werewolf lunged forward and buried its teeth into his stomach.

All the air in his lungs shot out, instantly rejected by his body. Harry thrashed not in any sort of attempt to get free or move away but only as involuntary reactions to his intestines being violently nudged, pulled, and torn away.

The beast snarled and attacked without regard for right or wrong, good or evil—only intent.

Bleeding out, unable to breathe, desperate for the end, Harry Pearson realized that he should have come here tomorrow morning instead, if he should have come at all. He was barely present mentally as the werewolf finally unleashed its stone-cold howl before lunging forward and ripping its mouth full of dagger-like teeth into his throat.

Harry's body thrashed and convulsed against its inevitable end.

His thoughts dimmed.

Eddie Cosby, Nina...rent...monster.

The End

Wetware
By
Tim Curran

WOLF-13

GERMANY: NACHTWALD,

U.S. ARMY RESEARCH FACILITY

BLACK FOREST, BADEN-WÜRTTEMBERG

MAY 1st, 12:02 AM

As the others staged in the shadowy corridor in their black tactical body armor, weapons at the ready, Bates tried to control his breathing, his spiraling mind. He was a man without nerves. He'd never understood fear until now, the way it could dig deep inside you, twist your guts into knots, undermine the very essence of your being.

Continue mission, a voice of authority whispered in his head. It was an old friend that had guided him through one ensanguined battlefield after another.

He tried to listen, but he could think only of Hayen.

The grotesque shape that leaped out of the darkness, a shaggy blur, a misshapen primordial form with slashing claws and an incapacitating feral stink, before anyone could even think of pulling triggers, Hayen's throat was torn out in a whirlwind of blood and macerated tissue that struck the wall like wet sleet.

Breathing in deeply, trying to calm himself, Bates stepped over Hayen's corpse. He pretended he couldn't see the spray pattern of blood, the red drops falling from the ceiling like rain.

"Let's get this done," he told the others. "Anything that moves is considered unfriendly."

Sure. That's all there is to it. That's how the game is played: find your target and remove it. Enough said.

He gave the signal and Pope and Friesen moved into the next room down the corridor.

"CLEAR!" they called out in unison.

Bates stepped in there. Administrative. An office of sorts. Very few places to hide. Still, he checked the closet, under the desks, every nook and cranny. His team looked at him like he was crazy.

Crazy and careful are not the same thing, he thought with a complete lack of amusement. He swallowed down his fear, repeated his mantra: *aim quick and aim sure, kneecap 'em, then aim for the head. Three shots. No more, no less.*

Out into the corridor again, the atmosphere of Nachtwald pressing down upon him: grim, sinister, and uninviting.

Another room: nothing. Just the rising sense that though the facility was empty, it was far from being unoccupied. As tac lights bracketed to carbines swept the corridor, shadows jumped over the walls. The team was terrified and he could see it in their eyes: white, stark fear. What they were up against here were not Islamic extremist shitheads or a homegrown redneck terror army. Those were known quantities that they had dispatched easily many times, this was something else, something out of a horror story.

The entire complex was a maze. It was like trying to navigate the warped byways of a lunatic's mind: one corridor led into another, labs and containment chambers, isolation tanks and rows of filthy cages that smelled like animal dens, except they were designed to hold human beings.

And what they did to them, oh Christ, what they created.

Bates had hunted men from Syria to Somalia to Afghanistan. He'd waded through blood and broken bodies, viewing carnage that would have made most people vomit, but it never bothered him. He ended every op with a glass of bourbon, a cigar, and a contented sigh of a job well done.

But this, *this.*

The corridor terminated at a T. Wolcek was on point, he deployed quickly when he got the signal from Bates. His tac light spiking before him, he moved into the left of the T at a low crouch. Then he screamed. There was a wet, meaty impact, followed by silence.

By the time the others got there, he was gone.

Taken.

Blood was splashed over the walls, dripping like a child's runny fingerpainting. His black Kevlar tactical helmet was spinning around and around on the floor. A smeared blood trail led up the corridor.

BLOOD RITES

12:13 AM

"MOVE!" Bates shouted. "GO! GO! GO!"

There was no attempt at stealth now, a killer was among them, picking them off, a sly and vicious predator that could tear a man apart in seconds and then fade into the shadows. They had to get it. They had to channel every ounce of horror and anger and killing fury they possessed into locating it and destroying it.

Nothing else mattered.

The team thundered down the corridor, following the blood trail. To the left, to the right, seemingly in circles. And then, and then.

Wolcek's carcass.

It looked as if it had exploded, a bag of meat that had erupted in all directions in a storm of macerated tissue, entrails, and blood. His remains were splattered on the walls, dripping from the ceiling, cast in a wide red sea of anatomy. One leg was wrenched free. His right hand was severed. Amazingly, it still gripped his carbine which glistened with fresh blood. His Kevlar vest was shredded, slashed open in a dozen places. Bates could not even imagine the strength and ferocity of the claws that accomplished something like that.

In Pope's flashlight beam was Wolcek's head. His left eye was missing, his jaws wrenched wide, tongue protruding pinkly. His face was gouged by four deep-cut ruts right down to the skull beneath.

Before anyone could comment on that or vomit out the contents of their queasy stomachs, a low, eerie howling echoed down the corridor, rising with volume and finally becoming a rasping, inhuman laughter.

Bates launched himself forward, running through Wolcek's blood pool. The others were with him, shriveling with terror but mainlining a mindless rage and the very real need for payback.

The beast waited for them.

In that split-second before the slaughter began in earnest, Bates saw it: not a man, not wolf, but a terrible hybrid of both. Its shaggy pelt was stained red, its massive snout dripping with blood as were the rapiers of its claws.

This was the Big Bad Wolf.

And it had come to kill them.

But it hadn't come alone.

There were five of them, possibly more. Men screamed as the lupine horrors leaped amongst them. Bodies dropped, faces were peeled from skulls, weapons were emptied, gigantic jaws tearing through flesh and crunching bone.

And then it was over.

Only Bates was left. His tac light revealed corpses sheared open, snipped in half like paper dollies. He pawed blood and stringy remains from himself. Dead men and dead wolves were scattered about, blasted apart by sustained fire.

He saw a distorted shape step from the consuming blackness. Its eyes gleamed scarlet, its ears laid back against its monstrous skull.

He tried to fire, but his magazine was empty.

Still, he jerked it, *click-click-click.*

The beast offered him a low, raw laughter, seized Friesen by the ankle and dragged him off into the darkness.

CQ ONE

PROVIDENCE, RI: DOUGLAS AVENUE,
SMITH HILL, NOVEMBER 10, 8:37 PM

In the darkness of the sedan, Bird held the IR monocular to his eye, studying the streets in the green field of the night-vision device. He saw a man come up the sidewalk, chin to his chest, hands stuffed in the pockets of his pants. It could have been just another homeless man, but he knew that it wasn't.

He smiled, handed the monocular to Olivia Adare. "I'm thinking, Pet, that we have ourselves a positive," he said in his smooth British accent. "Have a look then."

She snatched the monocular from him, studying the man on the walk. Physical description was close. But it was hard to be sure, the man they were looking for was thirty-two years old, muscular, clean-shaven. But after six months on the streets, living in gutters ...

"I'm not sure," she said.

"Be sure, Pet. That's our target. Trust me, you do trust me, don't you?" Bird said, grinning in the dark.

"About as much as I trust most snakes."

"Oh, how painful."

Trust Bird? Bird was CIA, a surveillance specialist. The Company had recruited him right out of British MI5, counterintelligence, where he had spent some fifteen years in Northern Ireland watching the IRA and assorted Loyalist paramilitary groups in conjunction with the SAS. He was good at his job. Too good, maybe. He had an almost supernatural ability to locate his target and an inhuman patience to study him/her/it in detail for weeks and months.

For the past three weeks they had been hunting the man on the sidewalk. Business as usual for Bird, but practically unbearable for Olivia who was a fountain of nervous energy.

"It's all in the mind-set," Bird told her. "You see, I am by nature not a man of action. Oh, perish the thought. If I wasn't watching targets, I'd be watching the telly. I am a man of non-action, a slug, a snail, and happily so. Like a stain, I rarely move. I become part of my environment, unremarkable, unnoticed, but I am watching. I am always watching."

Olivia studied the man on the sidewalk.

He paused at a trash can. He dug around in it even though he must have known that all the cans in this neighborhood were quite thoroughly plundered. But he came up with something he wanted: a half-smoked cigarette. He lit it up, then slowly scanned the streets.

And stopped.

Yes, stopped dead and she could feel his eyes on her. They were nearly half a block away in the dark and yet she could feel him looking at her. This more than anything else made her almost certain that this was their man. He turned away.

Olivia sighed. Maybe she was imagining things.

"Well, Pet," Bird said. "Shall we call it in? I await your decision as my superior."

"Stop calling me that," she said.

"Certainly, Pet."

This was all new to her. Before this she'd never been involved in CO, covert operations. She was a microbiologist by training and up until two months ago had been identifying possible bioterror threats for the NSA as part of a team that contained personnel from the CDC and the U.S. Army Medical Research Institute. The NSA had recruited her three years before and she left her position with the Department of Molecular Genetics and Virology at Baylor.

But two months ago, things had started happening.

Now she was hunting men.

She studied the man. Was he indeed the target? She had better be sure. Because if she called it in, this guy was in for a world of hurt.

Michael Steig, Born Syracuse, New York. Unmarried. No children. Eight-year veteran of the Army's 5th Special Forces Group. Two silver stars. Purple Heart. Distinguished Service Cross. A dozen other medals and commendations for clandestine work with CIA SAC/SOG, Special Activities Center/Special Operations Group.

A war hero.

A Green Beret.

And also a member of Wolf-13 ...

But Olivia didn't want to think about any of that. Wolf-13 was so classified and so obscene by nature that she refused to even consider it.

She kept watching the target.

He was Caucasian. *Check.* He did have an Army-issue fatigue jacket on. *Check.* But he was awfully thin, his beard shaggy, his hair long.

But it's been six months. People change, she told herself. *This guy has been on the run. Off the grid. He's been living like an animal, surviving as he was taught to survive.*

"Well?" Bird said.

Biting her lower lip, Olivia picked up her handheld radio, punched in the secure channel.

"Mother? Do you copy?"

"Mother copies. Go ahead," came the sexless voice.

"Mother this is CQ One," Olivia said. "Hunter's Moon"

There was a pause as the code was verified. "Hunter's Moon acknowledged, CQ One. Message?"

"Target is affirmative," she said. "Initiate Raptor. Repeat: initiate Raptor."

"Confirmed. Sequence initiated …"

MEAT

PROVIDENCE, RI: HAT'S PLACE,

DOUGLAS AVENUE, 8:42 PM

Tonight was a real graveyard, so James Hatly was glad to hear someone coming in for a sandwich or some eggs, *dear God, just don't let it be another crazy stewed on crank,* even it meant he'd have to wash a few dishes. Maybe it was Johnny Q or Stevie Coltrain coming in for some home fries and a couple over-easies, probably lost their asses shooting dice again.

No, just some white dude. Hat didn't like his looks, ragged and dirty, funny gleam in his eyes. This one was going to be trouble.

Homeless? Doped up? Psycho? Yeah, you get all kinds in this neighborhood.

So, Hat, though he was a good man, kind and decent to all people, put on some attitude, layered it on thick so maybe this crazy SOB would know he was in the wrong place at the wrong time, that Hat's Place wasn't a shelter offering handouts.

"Hell you want?" he asked, "We're closing."

This guy was oblivious: he just sat there on the stool, drumming his grimy hands on the Formica counter which was all scarred-up from old cigarette burns. His fingernails were long and discolored, filth packed under them as if he had been digging in dumpsters or rooting about in the soil.

Hat swallowed. His mouth felt suddenly very dry, a creeping unease spreading out in his belly. He wished somebody else would come in because he just did not want to be alone with this guy.

"I said we're closing," he tried again.

The guy stared into space with black, glossy eyes that were like windows looking onto some secret atrocity. He was a soldier boy, Hat figured, a vet. Had one of them Army coats, desert camouflage ... but dirty, worn, much like the man himself. His hair was filthy, clotted in greasy clumps, his beard long and tangled, the color of straw.

He looked up at Hat.

Ho, Jesus, look at those peepers.

Hat felt the streets run right out of him like piss down his leg. Those eyes. They could have burned holes through brick. The guy blinked, opened his hand and dropped a twenty on the counter.

"I need some food," he said in a scratching voice that was like a stick dragged through gravel.

Hat mopped a dew of sweat from his brow. "Closing up for the night, son. Give you a sandwich to go if you—"

"Meat," he rasped. "Want some meat."

Meat. That's what he said. Not I want a hamburger or a chop. Meat. Want some meat. And it was sure as hell not a request.

Hat swallowed but there wasn't enough water in Lake Michigan to moisten his throat. He was 53 years old. His wife, *old dear Raye, sweet as honey and soft as butter,* had died before her 25th birthday, leaving him all alone in the big, bad world to raise their children. And raise them he had. Not three streets away he had raised three sons and did it with a firm, sure hand, steering them away from drugs and crime and gangs, and no easy bit had that been. It meant being tough. Godawful tough sometimes. It meant backing down from no one to keep his boys safe and clean. And building up his café had meant the same thing. So, through the years he'd faced down some real animals to protect what was his.

But this guy, this guy had them beat.

Hat felt like Little Red Riding Hood scared shitless that the Big Bad Wolf was hiding behind a tree.

Except, dear Christ, he wasn't hiding at all.

"Said I want some meat," the guy said, getting ornery.

"Yes, sure." Hat made himself breathe. *Give him some fucking meat and get his psycho ass out of here.* "We got hamburgers, steaks, chops, chicken."

"Hamburger," the guy said.

Hat went at it. He got some nice fresh meat from the cooler and slapped it into patties. Nice ones.

Quarter-pounders. He got the grill going and made ready.

"Raw."

Hat turned, looked into those crazy eyes again, felt his skin crawl. "Did you say?"

"Raw. I'll eat 'em raw."

"Well, I don't know. There's state regs."

"Fuck the regs. I want 'em raw. Juicy."

Hat had a real bad feeling that he knew something about this guy, but what? *What?* Some kind of story making the rounds, wasn't it? Then he remembered. Sure. Some bullshit that Louis McKee was piping on about. Some crazy white guy living over at Ma Heller's place. *You know Ma's place, don't ya, Hat?* Louis said not a week back when he was trying to panhandle a few bucks. *Ma got this ofay motherfucker living down the basement. Dark and bad down there. Lots of rats. This white boy, he live down there. Crazy fucker. Remember Lawry Oates' boy? Marky? He was running with them Gangster Disciples, got his ass involved with a sister of some fucking Latin crew. They found him in a dumpster over to the Conception School. His ass was torn into little pieces, man. Except maybe it weren't the Latins that did him.* Louis was just a drunk. You couldn't believe what he said. *Catch this, Hat. Over to Ma's, some crazy fucker up on the roofs. Boys go up there, gonna kill his ass. They get there, he's gone. They hear a sound three rooftops away, a baying like a dog. They got the fuck out of there.* Crazy bullshit, that's all it was and Hat figured he had enough problems without spook stories.

Still, he moved quickly getting this guy his raw meat patties.

Soldier boy nearly grabbed them out of Hat's hands, started shoving them in his mouth, chewing them up. Blood and juice stained his beard, chunks of meat. He tore at it with teeth that were long and yellow.

"Need some more," the guy said. Again, not a request.

Hat, sweating and shaking, slapped out the patties fast as his hands would go and Soldier Boy, just crazy with it, made groaning and moaning sounds as he bit into the meat, getting it all over himself, on the counter. But it was never enough. He'd wolf it down, look back up at Hat with those black, soulless eyes, grinning with pink-stained teeth and reaching out with long bloody fingers.

"More," he said. "You hear me, *more.*"

Hat went at it and the patties disappeared one after the other. But then the supply was down to a pound and this crazy cracker had already eaten his way through eight pounds of raw meat and, Jesus, what was going to happen when the well ran dry?

Soldier boy was sucking juices from his fingers, grunting and puffing like he was getting off. Then he put his head down and started licking the blood from the countertop—*like an animal, like some kind of fucking animal*—and Hat did what he had to do: he grabbed Old Reliable from under the countertop, a battered Louisville Slugger that had kept the peace more than once, and cracked Soldier Boy right in the head with it. *Thunk!*

Soldier Boy was facedown on the counter, still breathing, but not moving.

Hat was watching his hands which were flat on the countertop to either side of his mangy head.

What the hell is this?

Those hands, still grubby, but covered in a fine red-brown fuzz now that was darkening, fingers growing long so that from index to pinkie they were all the same length

"Fucked up, didn't you? Guess it's self-serve now," Soldier Boy said, raising his head, his teeth grown long and sharp and his eyes a glossy blood-red.

And Hat, who'd seen some crazy, ugly shit in his time in the mean streets, let out a whimpering sound as Soldier Boy seemed to explode out of his clothes with a violent ripping noise, his anatomy changing and reconfiguring, his flesh melting and surging and boiling from the bones beneath, solidifying in the form of a gigantic wolf.

Now Hat really did piss himself.

The bat dropped from his fingers.

The wolf leaped over the counter, snarling and foaming with drool, its huge teeth gnashing together like carving knives. Hat held up a shaking hand instinctively and the wolf took it off right at the wrist with a slash of its curving black claws.

Then the wolf had him.

It grabbed him, all 250 pounds of him, raised him up and shook him around, blood jetting from the stump of his wrist. Then it forced him, face-first, right down on the grill and the agony was white-hot as his face sizzled and the flesh liquefied. When the wolf yanked him back up, most of his face was still on the grill, bubbling and burning, connected to his skull by blackened strings of tissue and red gristle. His melting eyes superheated and popped like fat ticks.

The wolf licked him with a barbed tongue, digging deeply into the cavity where his face had been. Then it tossed him against the wall with such force that his bones shattered on impact and left a dripping red splatter stain on the chalkboard where today's specials had been etched.

The wolf studied him, growling deep in its throat, and vaulted out the plate glass door without bothering to open it first.

RAPTOR

8:55 PM

The SAC/SOG spec ops team that burst from the back of the black tactical van was led by Niles, a twenty-two-year veteran of Delta Force and a cold-blooded killer by all accounts. His job was to eliminate the enemies of the United States and it was something he approached not only with a passionate zeal for life-taking, but an absolute fanaticism. Though in his own mind, particularly between missions when he spent his time quietly with his coin collection, he considered himself to be one of the nation's janitors, when the shit hit the floor, he was the first there to control and contain it, identity it *as* shat and bag it for further analysis.

He liked that. It was very detached, very harmless, very clinical.

But tonight, he was none of those things.

They had a target and it was another Wolf-13 subject—he did not use the word *monster,* nor any of the other pulp horror Lon Chaney monikers to identify them, and in Niles' mind, the target was an especially vile, steaming heap of scat that needed to be scooped up before the taxpayers caught a good whiff of it.

"We got visual," Osaki said over the encrypted net.

"Into position," Niles told him.

Marin and Hatch at his back, he moved forward down the alley with great stealth. The shadows made more noise than his team. Including himself, there were six of them outfitted in black fatigues and Kevlar vests.

Osaki was waiting for them at the bend.

With his NVGs, Niles could see metal dumpsters, garbage cans, skids of compacted cardboard ready for recycling. There were dozens of places to hide.

At a low crouch, he came around the bend with Osaki. Fowler was just ahead on point, scanning the darkness with his MP5.

"He's here," Fowler said. "We've got him boxed in. He moves fast. Gone before I get my sights on him."

"Let him play his card," Niles said, studying the long alleyway ahead, junk heaped everywhere, more garbage cans, pallets of barrels, dumpsters, piled lumber. "Don't let him draw you in."

From Steig's perspective, it was the perfect killzone, dark, shadowy, plenty of things to hide behind and to leap from. With his near-perfect night vision, he was probably watching them, studying their every move, already choosing the first throat he would tear out.

Not this time, you fuck, not this time, Niles thought, his hand reaching down for the tranquilizer gun at his hip. There was enough ketamine in the darts to drop a 600-pound tiger. He hoped it would be enough.

"Movement," Osaki said.

And it began.

BEAST WITHIN

9:04 PM

It knew the time had come.

Once again, it was a time of war and savagery and hunger. Every nerve ending in its body blazed hot with the need to kill, to satiate the blood-maddened beast within. There was no containing it. No controlling it.

The beast needed to slaughter.

To take lives and swim in pools of blood and reduce its prey to well-gutted husks. Breathing quickly with a low bestial rumbling, it went for the kill.

CAMO

9:06 PM

Osaki heard Niles over the net and as he was about to answer him, a shape vaulted out of the darkness, a blur, a satiny whisper of accelerated motion. He brought up his MP5, trying to track it but it was so damn fast.

It was here.

It was there.

It existed.

It did not exist at all.

He pivoted and fired a three-round controlled burst, just as he was trained. Then another. And another. And a second after his finger eased on the trigger, something hit him, slashed him, tore into him. The soft tissues of his throat seemed to explode in a hot, never-ending gush of dark blood.

He dropped to one knee, firing again with one hand as the other tried to stay the flow of blood from his neck. As he gasped for breath and black dots filled his head, he could hear the wet whistling of his sucking throat wound.

He pitched right over, still firing.

KILL ZONE

9:09 PM

The soldier had missed with nearly every round, but as he went down shooting, two rounds punched into the beast. They bit like teeth in its shoulder and ribs, channeling into its flesh, the slugs burning hot.

The others opened up, even though they did not have a clear target. By then, the beast was gone. Their rounds chewed into the brick wall but did no more damage.

The pain made the beast wary, but filled it with a wrath for killing that had to be satisfied. It would kill them all and peel the meat from their bones and it knew exactly how to accomplish this.

BODY COUNT

9:13 PM

Niles felt the discipline and cohesion of his team break down almost instantly. His men were firing at half-glimpsed shapes and shadows. Flashlight beams were strobing about like white swords, revealing a target for a split-second, then nothing at all.

Ambush.

Jesus, Steig had drawn them into a perfect kill zone. He called out for his men to retreat, but all they saw was Osaki's heaped form on the ground, blood spreading out from it, and they wanted payback anyway they could get it.

"PULL BACK!" Niles cried over the encrypted net. "PULL THE FUCK BACK!"

Too late.

Not four feet from him, Fowler grunted and dropped his weapon. Blood spattered in Niles' eyes. He pawed it away with one leather glove and his light showed him Fowler laying there, twitching. His face had been torn right off the skull.

Shit.

The beast moved among them: leaping, hopping, slashing, biting, clawing. Nothing could move that fast or with such deadly precision.

Marin let out a scream and fired blindly, seeking a target that did not exist. Niles hit the ground so he didn't get cored by a stray round. Hatch wasn't so lucky. A ricochet caught him in the knee and a three-round burst from Marin caught him full-on in the face. He spun in a circle, blood erupting from his eyes and ruptured jaw and the flap of cartilage that had been his nose.

Friendly fire.

Niles turned and saw Marin's MP5 clatter to the ground, but he was gone. A mist of blood filled the air. It sprayed and gushed, striking Niles like a sudden summer squall.

For the briefest of instants, he saw the beast standing atop a pile of bailed cardboard. It had Marin by the throat, holding him like a doll.

Niles knew he couldn't fire without hitting the man, but he had no choice. He brought up his weapon and something spinning end over end, a hulking shape, struck him and his shots went wild.

It was Marin's disemboweled carcass.

It hit him, flattened him, and by the time he shoved it away, the beast was hovering over him. He went for his 9mm sidearm, but the beast made a noise very much like harsh, croaking laughter and slashed his hand to ribbons. The pain was intense and Niles knew he was going to die, but he would not give the beast the satisfaction of hearing him cry out or beg for mercy.

He crawled maybe five feet and the beast stomped on his back.

"Fuck, you," Niles managed.

That cold, calculating semi-laughter again. The beast seized him by the throat and lifted him up into the air at eye-level, breathing its hot, rank breath on him. With its other paw (or was it a hand?), it slit open his Kevlar vest and then opened his belly until his small intestines bulged out.

Then it dropped him.

He was allowed to crawl another five or six feet, dragging his viscera, before it stomped him again. And then, without further ado, it ripped his head off.

PREY

9:15 PM

Now the beast stood at the mouth of the alley, its huge chest rising and falling. It tossed Niles' head into a dumpster and licked his blood off its claws.

The soldiers were all dead.

It knew this.

Yet, there was something that made it uneasy. There were others. He could smell them, their fear scent, the ripe chemical cocktail of their hormones and juicing endorphins.

At the end of the block, there was a black sedan.

In it, the beast knew, were enemies.

BODY BAGS

9:34 PM

"Mother? Mother? This is CQ One. Do you copy?" Olivia Adare said over the secure channel, trying to keep the rising panic from her voice. "Mother? Do you copy?"

There was only static coming in over the radio. Bird looked over at her in the darkness of the car and for once there were no pithy comebacks or humorous anecdotes with his trademark dry delivery. His eyes shined in the green glow of the instrument cluster like those of a frightened rabbit.

Olivia swallowed. "Mother, this is CQ One. Please respond. This is high priority."

Again, static. It felt like she was trembling inside, as if something at her very core was squirming. They had been monitoring the Raptor team and things had been getting problematic, and now just dead air. Something had happened and she feared the very worst. If the Raptor team was wiped out and Mother was offline, it meant they were on their own against Michael Steig, or the predatory thing he now was. The very idea was disturbing.

"Mother here."

Olivia outlined the situation quickly. "Please advise, Mother."

"Standby, CQ One."

"Standby, she says. Oh, bloody hell, Olivia, I think it's time for some common-sense evasion," Bird said. "Let's get the hell out of here."

He barely finished the sentence when Olivia let out a muffled cry as she saw a gargantuan form outside the passenger side window. There was a blur of movement, a devastating impact that rocked the sedan, then the window behind Bird exploded inwards in a single spiderwebbed sheet.

He screamed.

She went for her sidearm as she caught a glimpse of a huge slavering mouth full of teeth. Then two clawed hands seized Bird and pulled him out into the night, or at least far enough so that jaws with huge fangs speared into his throat. Bird spasmed, legs kicking, a gurgling cry coming from him as the beast roared and its jaws clamped down, a severed artery spraying loops of blood into the car that looked black as ink.

Olivia had her 9mm in hand, but there was no way she could shoot as she'd been trained without hitting Bird and a voice in her head screamed hysterically, *help us, help us, oh Jesus, somebody please help us,* as she threw her door open and tried to draw a bead on the creature that had Bird in its jaws and was shaking him violently like a terrier with the broken body of a rat.

She fired once and missed.

Blood sprayed from Bird's gored throat and a jet of it wetted down her face and hair.

Now the beast had Bird in its hands, hoisting him high in the air and there was no possibility he was still alive. Olivia fired again, catching the beast in the shoulder, but it didn't even slow it down. It smashed Bird into the roof of the car again and again and each time it did, there was a sloppy, wet cracking like the wishbone of a chicken being pulled apart.

Olivia fired two more times at the shaggy shape and then it threw Bird's body at her. She ducked underneath it and it struck the curb, bones shattering. Bird rolled over, his face a mask of blood, one eye jutting from its socket like that of a decompressed deep-sea fish.

Then the beast was gone.

No, it was to her left.

She fired.

To her right.

She fired.

Then she was half-running, half-stumbling, smelling the pungent feral stink of the beast as it seemed to close in from every direction at once. She was knocked to the pavement, her gun lost, screaming and crying as she waited for the jaws to end her life.

Then the creature jumped on her back, forcing her down, and did the most awful thing: it spoke to her, breathing a perfectly nauseating hot, raw meat stink in her face.

"Now just where in the hell do you think you're going?"

And then it dragged her off into the night.

WET WORK

9:53 PM

For Bates, it never really ended, he was the only survivor of the raid on Nachtwald in the Black Forest. And every time he closed his eyes, the events of that terrible night played out again and again, the trauma fresh and no less devastating for the passage of six months.

He remembered.

He could do nothing *but* remember his team being wiped out by monsters that were nearly impossible to kill or evade.

He saw the beast take Friesen.

The team—Hayen and Pope and Wolcek and the others, were all dead, their gutted carcasses spread over the floor.

In the beams of dropped tactical lights, the beast paused with Friesen and looked right at him. Its eyes were bright blood-red like those of a South American tree frog and as it watched him, he saw that they never blinked. Like a snake's, they seemed to be covered in a translucent nictitating membrane so that it was constantly watching, constantly aware of its surroundings.

He was out of his mind by that point, juiced on pure, unreasoning terror, his finger reflexively jerking the trigger of his tactical carbine even though the magazine was empty. The beast could only be one thing and a childhood of horror comics and bad movies informed him instantly as to what that was: a werewolf.

It could be nothing else.

Its sleek, well-muscled body was pale gray and oddly smooth, covered in a barely-discernable fuzz, but its huge head was that of a wolf, a great shaggy mane of fur falling over its shoulders and running down its back. Its hands were nearly human, though gnarled and clawed, scarred and scabbed from the hunt.

As it looked at him, he thought of the fighting knife at his belt, but the idea of pulling it was ludicrous, it would have been like facing off against a Siberian tiger with a nail file.

The beast seemed to be grinning at him. It uttered a low, dog-like snarl deep in its throat, an amused sound as if it knew there wasn't a damn thing he could do to stop it. Thin black lips pulled away from fangs like yellow ivory speckled pink from its feedings. Loops of bloody saliva dangled from its mouth.

It could smell the fear on him and he knew it.

It was something its kind inspired in their victims and the bouquet was immensely pleasing to it.

Bates came out of it, sitting in his truck some distance away from CQ One's abandoned sedan and the mutilated remains of Bird. Though the air in the cab was cold and he could see his breath in the November chill, hot sweat beaded his face, steaming.

He had been rogue six months now since the CIA cut him loose after the events at Nachtwald. He was told that he had a breakdown. He was forcibly interred at a military psychiatric facility where they picked at his brain, drugged him with antipsychotics, and put him through a program of behavior modification. When he finally told them what they wanted to hear, that none of it had really happened, they released him with a full pension.

But he had been on the hunt since.

No longer with the Company, he still had plenty of high-level contacts, and it was through them he tracked the surviving members of Wolf-13 *and* the operatives that tracked them.

And I'll get them, I'll kill everyone of the werewolves, and nothing can stop me.

He still did not know the exact specifics of Wolf-13, how such an obscenity was engineered, he only knew that its members had fought in the Gulf and he could just about imagine how many enemies of the

United States they had vanquished, how many terror cells were disrupted by savage, monstrous things that stalked the night.

It's time, he told himself. *The trail is still fresh.*

Though his heart rate was accelerated, his blood pressure high, he calmed himself, telling himself that this was the one he wanted most of all. The one that had stared him down in Nachtwald. Its name was Michael Steig and tonight it would die.

He pulled off a flask of Jim Beam, steeling himself. He checked the connections on the vest he wore beneath his overcoat. All was ready.

Steig.

Goddamned Steig.

The way he had looked at him, emasculating him, making him feel not like a man but some scurrying prey animal. *Him.* A guy who had dozens of bodies out there, a man who was beyond fear.

But he had not been beyond it that night.

As the beast looked at him with those neon-bright red eyes, it had made another sound: a guttural sort of laughter that went right up his spine in chill waves. It knew that he knew he was helpless against it. Its bloodflecked snout seemed to be grinning. It was pleased with itself and looked on him with contempt as a weakling, a bug it could crush anytime it amused it to do so, a trapped fly whose wings it would pluck free on a whim.

Again, that terrible laughter when he opened his mouth to speak and all that came out was a dry hissing sound.

Then it dragged Friesen away, joining the other werewolves that were tearing apart what remained of his team. In the glow of the tac lights, it went to work on him. It split him open, yanking out his intestines and shattering his ribcage to get at the juicy mass of his heart. Then it slashed and tore until it found his liver and pulled it out by the roots. It bit into it, first almost delicately like an epicure, then with a violent, wolfish hunger.

Out of his mind, Bates sat there, listening to them feed, licking the skins of his men free, sucking their blood and crunching their bones in massive jaws. And all the while, making a revolting purring noise like lions with their kills.

He stepped from the truck.

Many lights had come on in the neighborhood as people wondered if all the shooting was some gang-related incident. At the sedan, Bates slid on a pair of infrared goggles.

Yes, the blood was easy to follow. The beast had left a perfect trail as it made off with the woman. On a chill night, the hot blood prints were the perfect spoor.

Now, Steig.

Tonight.

Bates moved off to his destiny and the climax of many months of careful work.

ABDUCTED

PROVIDENCE, RI: CHALKSTONE AVENUE,

WANSKUCK, NOVEMBER 10, 11:27 PM

When Olivia came out of it, her back was up against some kind of beam, her head slumped forward. She was tied up, wrists bound. Her head ached where the beast had struck her, putting her lights out. She was bruised, beaten, every muscle cramped and aching, but she seemed to be whole.

At least for the time being.

Wherever she was, it was pitch black. The beast could have been mere feet away.

No, no, you'd smell it. Nothing smells like they do—that wild, gamey, blood-and-meat slaughterhouse smell.

Quietly, carefully, she tried to loosen her wrists, but it was impossible. There was no wiggle room. Steig had her right where he wanted her. He had let her live and there had to be a reason for that, something she felt would be unbearably ugly.

Breathing.

She wasn't alone then. He was close, but not too close. Maybe twenty feet, if that. There was a scratching sound and a match was struck, the glow of its flame nearly blinding. A gas lantern was lit, chasing away the shadows and revealing her captor who stood by an old wooden table, completely naked.

"I see you're with us again," he said.

Olivia said nothing. She thought about Wolf-13 and how the surviving members had escaped from the research facility in Baden-Württemberg after they had wiped out the spec ops team. How they had been tracked down one by one and destroyed, except for a few. But mostly she thought about Michael Steig, whom they had been looking for all these months and what he was, what he was capable of.

"Feel free to speak," he said. "I'm hardly a monster."

Sick humor, particularly with all the lives he had taken and what he had done to Bird. Poor, loveable, funny Bird with his sixth sense and eagle eye. A coward at heart, but an absolute professional at what he did.

She watched Steig, terrified, yet intrigued that she was finally face to face with him: a monster, a predator, a blood-lusting creature straight out of folklore.

He stood there, studying her with a crooked half-smile on his mouth. She didn't think she'd ever met anyone that was so comfortable with their nakedness. There was something very disturbing about that, something natural and primal about him. And she knew what that something was, even though she preferred not to give it a name. He was well-muscled, darkly handsome, and she supposed under ordinary circumstances she would have found him more than a little appealing, but not here, not with what was about to happen. His body was bruised and scarred, though amazingly hairless. Crusted with filth and old bloodstains. His eyes gleamed like glass balls and his teeth were long and yellow. Even in his human form, he was a wolf.

"You're wondering why I haven't killed you," he said.

She swallowed with some difficulty. "It crossed my mind."

"Because you know who I am and, perhaps, *what* I am, so I want to tell you a story. Would you like to hear it?"

"Yes."

He laughed with a dry, grating sound. "You're lying. All you want is to get out that door and run." He shrugged. "No matter. Listen to my story; you'll find it entertaining."

His story concerned, of all things, a Hungarian serial killer named Bela Kiss who murdered a number of women, drained their blood, and packed their bodies in casks of alcohol. None of this was known until later when Kiss was off fighting in World War I and the remains were discovered. A manhunt was undertaken to apprehend him, but he slipped away every time. He had joined the war effort to procure fresh corpses to slake his appetite for human flesh.

"He was," Steig said, "what you might call a member of my tribe, though he came to it quite honestly, the affliction being passed down his bloodline from primeval times, I would imagine." He lit a cigarette and blew out a rolling cloud of smoke. "You see, the Hungarian authorities claimed that he was killed during the war, but that wasn't so. His crimes of cannibalism and lycanthropy on the battlefield were discovered, so he was captured and placed in a secure military prison. Living in a dark cell and subsisting on raw meat, his existence was a closely-guarded secret."

Sometime after the Soviet Union collapsed and the Iron Curtain came down, Kiss, then well over a hundred years old, but looking barely forty, was procured in a joint effort by American and British intelligence. He was taken to a high-security facility in Germany's Black Forest where his genetics were carefully harvested for the next twenty years.

"And that, you see, is how Wolf-13 was born. We were all Special Forces, willing guinea pigs, carefully selected to become the ultimate soldiers. It was done through transgenics: Bela's genes were introduced to our genomes and, well, you know what the result was, don't you? Ah, yes, *werewolves.* My DNA is a wetware program."

"That's fantastic," she said.

He laughed. "Oh, stop, you knew most of this. I know who you are. What your background is. Who you work for. Let's not pretend. Though I do appreciate such a captive audience while I unburdened the trauma of my soul." He took one last pull of his cigarette and then dropped it, crushing it out with his heel. "Now what to do with you." He licked his lips. "Particularly when I find you so very tempting."

"You could let me live. I wouldn't tell them where you are."

"Yes, you would. Again, let's not pretend. And I won't pretend that you don't make hungry." He stepped closer. "You see, human beings are our cattle, our sheep. You are a lamb and I am a wolf. You are steak and I am the knife that cuts you. My destiny is to cut and yours is to *be* cut."

Olivia shook her head frantically from side to side. "Please, I, oh please."

"Enough," he said and his voice had dropped a couple octaves until it had nearly the tonal quality of a dog's bark. "Watch now: pay attention. I'm going to show you the purest form of technology in existence: organic technology. Now you'll see how this wetware works."

Despite herself, Olivia groveled and pleaded, she sobbed and cried out, even begged, but it did no good. This was endgame. No one would save her from her horrible fate. It was preordained, it was destiny, just as he claimed.

His entire body seemed to flicker like a candle flame, mutating, distorting out of shape, his flesh becoming a viscid, crawling mass. He throbbed and boiled, roiling like boiling magma, realigning with a grisly wet popping and solidifying into a hunched-over goblin, a living abomination. His skin was pale gray and taut over a jutting subhuman skeleton rippling with muscle and lightly furred with silky silver fuzz. Thick, greasy, tangled fur draped from his wolf's head and shoulders and spilled over his upper torso. His fingers became knobby, elongated digits set with hooked black claws.

He shifted from one life form into another in what seemed seconds: a naked man becoming the Big Bad Wolf.

Huge, lucent eyes the color of blood clots stared out from his lupine head, jaws opening and opening until it seemed like they could swallow the world, a black tongue flicking over yellow tusk-like teeth. *"Pretty slick, eh?"* he said in a guttural voice like the low growl of a man-eating lion.

Olivia was not just overwhelmed with horror, but devastated by it. She shook. Her limbs quaked. Hot/cold sweat ran down her face. Her teeth chattered. Somewhere during the process, her bladder had emptied itself.

The wolf seemed aware of it, too, sniffing the air excitedly and moaning in its throat. *"I hunger,"* it said. Then it froze, cocking its head. It held up one hand, the fingers splayed, light gleaming off its talons. *"But, wait. We have a visitor."*

It stood fully erect, lips peeling back from teeth that gnashed together like cutlery. It took two more steps in Olivia's direction, then it gripped its penis and squirted hot urine over her, splashing her hair and face. She shrieked as it burned her eyes and singed her sinus membranes.

Then the beast went down on its his knees before her. *"A kiss to remember me by,"* it snarled and ripped the ropes that held her, shearing them easily. As she made to crawl free, it gripped her left wrist and bit into it. She screamed as it lapped up the flow of blood until its teeth were pink with it.

PRIMAL SCREAM

11:55 PM

"You followed the trail as I knew you would," the wolf said, immensely pleased with itself. *"Bait offered and bait taken. Now I have you as I should have had you six months ago."*

Bates stepped into view, staring at the horror not ten feet from him. This was it. This was what he'd been waiting for. This was the monster that had destroyed his team, his friends, his comrades. He had waited so long for this moment. Now there would be payback, now there would be a final and necessary retribution. The wolf thought it had baited him, drawn him in, but it was most certainly the other way around.

"You've come to die," said the wolf. *"How noble, how very heroic."*

Bates did not argue. "Yes, I've come to die and to kill."

The wolf was unfazed by what it no doubt perceived as its visitor's enigmatic comments. The threat of his words was lost and mostly because the wolf did not fear human beings: they were prey, but they were not equals in combat.

Bates knew this.

Since he was released from the bughouse and pensioned out, he had actively hunted the members of Wolf-13 and he had killed two of them. And in each case, he accomplished this by turning their own arrogance and supreme confidence against them.

He looked over at the woman sprawled on the floor. She was CIA. He knew that. Had she been taken here to fill Steig's larder or simply for mating?

The werewolf was getting ready to attack and he knew it, it was hunched-over, hands held out before it, nails made ready for disemboweling and fangs unsheathed for throat-ripping. Classic battle stance.

Bates grinned. "Well, come on then."

The wolf growled with a terrible rumbling thunder and charged. With nothing but a knife in his hand, Bates met it. There was a collision of bodies and thrashing limbs, the wolf was stabbed and slashed quite effectively, but not enough to stop its claws from laying open its human adversary or its muzzle from snapping meat from his face. It was blood and war, a primeval contest of cutting and slashing, biting and snarling, shouting and channeled death and brute strength.

But the wolf won, of course.

Bloodied, torn, skin peeled and hanging, sheaths of muscle laid open, arteries gushing, Bates hung limp in the embrace of the monster. Both were injured, both in incredible pain, but only one had the hyper-charged metabolism to heal.

"And now I have you, don't I, little man?" the wolf said, its snout stained red, one eye slit open and oozing drainage.

"Do you?"

One broken hand fished inside his ragged coat and pulled the detonation cord of the white phosphorus bomb pack strapped beneath his body armor. The wolf seemed to sense death and annihilation at the last possible second as the bomb went off, the explosion throwing both man and beast twenty feet through the shell of the abandoned warehouse where they crashed into a heap of stacked, moldering lumber. But by then, of course, both were engulfed in hissing, incinerating phosphorus and they blazed like match heads, burning brighter and brighter and brighter.

Bates died nearly instantly, but the wolf struggled on as it burned, its survival instinct refusing death, crashing finally to the floor in a blackened, carbonized mass that sputtered and popped and let out greasy black plumes of smoke as the phosphorus continued to cremate its remains.

And by then, the warehouse had become an inferno.

WETWARE

NOVEMBER 11, 12:04 AM

Olivia was knocked ten feet herself by the initial concussion and blowback of the explosion. Singed, banged-up, coughing and gagging, she crawled over the floor until she found the door and fell out of it into the night, smoke funneling after her. The fresh air invigorated her and she continued to drag herself across the weedy parking lot until the warehouse was behind her. It continued to burn.

But she was alive.

Her hands and face were blistered, the hair burned off half of her head. Her coat hung in rags, burnt and smoking.

Alive, oh God, yes, I'm alive and I'll stay alive.

Shock. She worried that she was in shock because she should have been in much more pain than she was, yet, she felt more alive than she ever had in her life.

But then she knew why.

As she lay there, battered and scorched, the night's events like some lopsided dark fantasy peeled from an equally lopsided nightmare, she knew very well what even then was inside her, changing her, regressing her, making her a creature of the night and shadows from an evil fairy tale.

She smelled the night and everything that lived, hunted, and existed within it. She scented blood and beating hearts and the flesh she began to hunger for, red and well-marbled.

Wetware, she thought then, something all-too human cringing inside her. *Wetware.*

Then it was gone and her primal appetites and instinctual drives were on full display. Content, restless, and hungry, she raised her towards the black, fuming sky and howled at the moon high above.

The End

Almost Never
By
Edward Lee

crunch

Katie took another step, then froze, listened.

crunch

Just a tiny sound, from the trees behind her. Perhaps she'd imagined it; Grandpa always said she had a big imagination. But then--a rustle? Did she hear a voice? Katie's heart fluttered.

crunch, crunch

She broke briskly down the narrow, tree-lined trail, taking long strides over fallen branches and gnarled roots. Around her, the woods seemed too still, too quiet. The moon, just rising, dappled her little face in white light. The grocery bag under her arm felt like a satchel of dead weight.

Those two men, she realized. She'd noticed them several times, following her around in the store. Now, the faster she walked, the more aware she became of the soft, quick crunching behind her that could only be footsteps...

***

"Someone's been following me, Grandpa." The flimsy screen door snapped shut. Katie rose on her tiptoes to set the bag of groceries on the counter.

"What's that, honey?" Grandpa wheeled forward, keen at the sudden question. "You say someone's been-_"

"Two men. I've seen them in the grocery store a few times, and I think they've been following me down the trail." Her small confused face turned to the old man. "Why would two grownups want to follow me?"

Grandpa's aged visage seemed to twitch; his knuckly hands tightened on the rungs of the wheelchair. *Blast it,* he thought. *Two men.* Jesus. He and his granddaughter didn't bother anyone. Why couldn't people leave them alone? "You just steer clear of them, honey," he said. "From now on, I'll do the shopping. You just stay here where it's safe."

"Grandpa!" she little girl scoffed. "You can't get to the store in your wheelchair. The trail's not big enough."

"I'll get on all right, don't you worry. I'm not as useless as people might think," Grandpa complimented himself. "What you got to understand, honey, and it's a sad thing, but, see, there're a lot of bad people in this world, evil people." He gulped thickly at the thought. "People who'd want to do bad things to a little girl like you."

Katie began to put the groceries away, oblivious in her innocence. "What kind of things, Grandpa?"

"Never you mind about that." God, what a question! How could he explain something like that to a little girl? *There shouldn't be no need to explain,* he retorted to himself. *'Cos such things just shouldn't be.* "You just do like your old granddad tells ya. I'll be able to get this blasted chair down the trail. Might take awhile,but I'll manage. Old duff like me could use the exercise."

"*Grand*pa." Katie stretched the word. "That's dumb. I can get there in ten minutes."

"And I don't want no more said about it, you hear me, miss?" No, he could never explain. Never. Child molesters, pedophiles. *Creatures,* he thought. They were out there, everywhere. His disgust seemed to percolate in his head, like pitch bubbling. He watched Katie bend to place the steaks and nonesuch in the refrigerator. She seemed radiant in her naivete, springy and slim in the simple avacado dress and flipflops. She was a lone flower in a vast field of parasites. Bright white-blond hair hung long and straight to the middle of her back, several strands of which swayed before her unblemished face. The old man's heart felt squashed, in the sure knowledge that it was her innocence that made her such easy prey for all the evil in the world.

***

"We shoulda nabbed her tonight," Binny said, peering forward through low branches. "Why piss away time? The sooner we get her upstate, the sooner we got our scratch."

Cementhead, Rocco concluded. "I told you, it's supposed to rain tonight. That's a dirt road we're parked on back there. The van'd leave treadmarks. And you left your damn gloves on the console, as usual."

Binny shrugged, as though the observation were of no significance whatsoever. "So what? We're gonna torch the place. What I need gloves for?"

Rocco was no crime tech but he wasn't stupid. In the joint, you hear about the latest. "They got lasers now, man, and special lights, and some new resin stuff that can lift prints ten years old off charred wood and metal. Our mitts are both on file and you know it. We'd be boy-cunt before we could even blink. We'd both have size-11 assholes by the time we got out." Rocco had already done a nickel in the cut; an abduction rap would put him away for twenty, easy. Binny must've lost half his brain the last time he took a shit. *No way I'm going back to the cut on account of this numbskull.* It wasn't something he ever talked about, but during his nickel, he'd taken it up the backway a few times himself—it felt like taking a Thanksgiving shit in reverse--and he'd sucked more his share of balony ponies too. Half the guys in a fed cut were buttons for the big families in Philly. You fuck with one of *those* guys, you're dead before chow call.

"Yeah, talk about a cake walk," Binny assessed, ignoring his partner's cautions. They'd staked the place out good a couple of times already, and had the routine down pat. Just about every night at seven sharp the kid would take the trail around the woods to the Safeway, pick up groceries, and walk back. A cute little girl, real young, like eight or nine. *The old guy in the chair must have some real dogshit for brains letting a kid that age walk the woods at night,* Rocco speculated. Some people just didn't get it, did they?

Rocco had run up some high markers at the wrong places; even bad guys had bad days. He'd taken five large from shylocks to win back his dump, and hit a losing streak. The shylocks had been Vinchetti's men. They gave him a choice, since he was from the neighborhood and only had one stint on his rap sheet. "You can feed the fish, or you can work for Vinchetti." Rocco didn't like the water. They'd set him up with Binny, to run errands for Vinchetti's lieutenant in Maryland, and to "make grabs." They'd pulled a dozen so far. Malls seemed best, and the safest, but this... Even Rocco had to agree. A cake walk. They couldn't ask for an easier grab. *Almost too easy,* he thought, hunkering down beside Binny, who roved the lit windows with a small pair of Bushnell's. The squat little house sat way back in the woods, off one of the old county logging tracks. No car, no outside lights, no neighbors. From what they could make of the place, there wasn't even a telephone, and it was just the old guy and little girl. Probably the usual story; the kid's folks croak in a car wreck, or maybe mom leaves town with the plumber, and dad takes a bullet in the Gulf thing, so now the geezer's taking care of the kid. And the kid...

Rocco's belly squirmed.

"Would you gander that little peach, man," Binny remarked. The scumbag actually licked his lips. "Vinchetti'll pay double for that kind of soft stuff."

"Why?"

"She's blond. The Yaks pay big money for blond kids that aren't beat."

Yaks referred to the Japanese mob, and beat, in this business, meant that the kid wasn't over twelve. He'd seen some of the shit himself once or twice; sometimes they helped Vinchetti's crew set up when they made a delivery. Rocco had about puked. He was no saint, sure--a pinch, a fence, he'd even run skag in the 70's--but this shit drew the line. Rocco, after all, was born Catholic.

"I was thinking of getting out," he said.

Binny shot him a funky look. "Getting out of what?"

"This whole gig, man. I don't like it. I mean, we're talking about kids, for Christ's sake."

"You ain't getting out of nothing." Binny went back to the binoculars. "Your marker's clean only for as long as you grab for Vinchetti, so don't be stupid. You walk out on him, paisan, and they'll find you the next day in some apartment project laundry room looking like a platter of cold cuts, and they'll blow-torch your cock off for starters."

Rocco frowned. This was probably true. He'd never met Vinchetti--aka Vinnie Shorteyes, on account of he had an eye for short stuff. Vinchetti ran the kiddie porn circuit all along the east coast. What they did was they grabbed kids and used them for videos, then they'd sell the kids to their dope honchos overseas, the Japs, the Burmese. They'd flick the kids on 1/4-inch masters, then dupe the masters and send them out to their lab mail-drops for mass-reproduction. The feds called it "The Underground," and it was a big market. Lot of times, Rocco couldn't sleep. He'd seen the kids' faces, the terror in their eyes, the innocence. He couldn't bear to think of what went on in their heads while Vinchetti's crew set up the cameras and the lights...

"Kids," he muttered. "Christ. Kids."

"Shut up, man," Binny sniped. "You're starting to sound like a stool. If we don't do it, someone else will-- fact of fucking life. Besides, we'll bag five grand a pop on this little nookie." Binny looked up, grinning in the dark. "Five grand. That's righteous bucks if you ask me. Shit, we'd be on the street taking down candy stores if Vinchetti hadn't dropped this gig in our laps. And you remember the last guy who tried to book on him? They picked him up in Jersey, autopsied the guy alive in a Red Roof Inn. Then they cut off the fucker's face and fed-exed it to his mother..."

Rocco's mouth went dry. That would be some party. *Thank God my mother's dead,* he thought.

Binny rambled on, "Plus I gotta feeling we're gonna bag more than five large on this one. The old fucker gives the kid cash whenever she goes to the store. You ever see her stop at the bank? He's probably one of these old-fashioned old cranks who doesn't believe in banks. Keeps his life's savings in a gym bag under the bed or some shit. We're gonna be walking with some green here, paisan."

Rocco felt distant, barely hearing the words. All he could see just then, and all he could think about...were the kids . . .

"And I say we take them out tonight, right now."

Rocco ground his teeth. "No way they're sending me up on a kiddie porn bust. I told you, it's gonna rain. We'll leave evidence all over the place."

Binny opened his mouth, to complain further, when suddenly the sky broke. A moment later, it was teeming.

"Okay, man," Binny gave in. "So we do it tomorrow night, then. No ifs, ands, or buts. Got it?"

***

"Grandpa?"

Katie leaned over, gently nudged the old man.

"Hey, Grandpa?"

He sat sound asleep in the chair, his head lolled to one side. Katie didn't have the heart to wake him; he was old, he needed his rest. Yesterday, he'd forbidden her to go shopping, but... *I'll go,* she decided. *He can't go. In the chair? It'd take hours!*

Grandpa kept his money behind the kitchen baseboard; Katie plucked out a $20 bill and replaced the board. A long time ago, he'd turned his money into T-bills, whatever they were, and once a year a special cab came out to the house and took him to town where he cashed in some interest. Katie wasn't sure what interest was, either, not that it mattered. Grandpa was a good man, and he always made sure there was enough money for things.

It was already dark when she embarked, dressed in her Smurfs shirt, flipflops, and spangled pants. It would be getting cold in a month or so, and Katie worried about that. Grandpa had some problem where his hands hurt in the cold. With that, and the chair, he had enough problems. The least Katie could do was go to the store.

She moved briskly down the narrow trail through the woods. An owl hooted; moonlight shimmered in the trees. As she quickened her pace, her fine blond hair rose behind her like an aura.

Her big eyes fixed ahead. She remembered what Grandpa said, about how there were some people who would want to do bad things to a little girl like her. Katie didn't understand what those things could be, but that only distressed her more deeply. *Why can't everybody be good?* she ineptly wondered. She and Grandpa never did bad things. *Why would people want to do bad things to us?*

At the grocery store, her heart quickened as she wandered the aisles. She always checked for the things that were on sale. A special on ground beef. Window cleaner two for the price of one. And laundry detergent. She chose the store brand because it was a quarter cheaper than Tide. She knew she was hurrying. She felt antsy and weird in the express line. She wanted to get out of there, and back to the house before Grandpa woke up.

On the way back she failed to notice the big white windowless van parked just off the utility road.

She felt watched all the way back down the trail. She knew she hadn't imagined those two men. Several times when she'd been shopping, they'd followed her around the store, always stopping and turning when she looked back. But they weren't there tonight, she happily realized. Nor did she hear any sounds behind her as she walked the trail. Katie suddenly smiled. They must be gone! Yes, the two men must've gone away, gone to follow someone else.

Katie's smile widened. She skipped back to the house, happily toting her bag of groceries.

***

"Blast it, Katie!" Grandpa railed, leaning forward in the chair. "I told you not to go to the store! I told you--"

"Don't worry, Grandpa," Katie cut in.

"Don't worry! How am I supposed to not worry with that pair of weird ones followin' you around?"

Katie closed the door and began to put away the groceries. "You were asleep, Grandpa. I didn't want to wake you up. And besides, those two men are gone."

Grandpa's stern visage laxed a bit, and he eased back into the chair. "You mean they weren't followin' you tonight?"

"Nope," Katie was happy to inform. "And they weren't at the store either. They're gone."

Grandpa considered this. "Well. Hmm. Maybe they are, but you still shoulda woke me up. Can't be too careful, not these days."

Katie's young face beamed at her grandfather. "Don't worry, Grandpa. I told you. Those men are gone. I'm sure of it."

***

"Yeah, I'm sure of it," Binny acknowledged, focusing the binoculars from their low lookout in the trees. "It's a gas stove, all right. Makes the place easier to torch."

Rocco's face felt like a mask of wood. He had the timer ready to go, a simple rig yet an ever-reliable one-- a metal-case watch with a plastic face strapped around a six-volt drycell battery. You tape the positive lead to the watch casing, and the negative to a thin nail melted through the plastic face. A piece of Jetex had been tied between the leads. When the minute hand made contact with the nail (the watch had no second hand) the circuit was made, the Jetex burned off at 800 degrees, and BOOM!

Rocco, however, wasn't thinking of pyrotechnics at this precise moment. He'd dreamed again last night, of the bleak faces of the children, of their vacant thousand-yard stares. *This is some bad shit,* he very simply thought. In a queer moment of vertigo, he looked at the back of Binny's head. God, it would be so easy. Rocco packed a Smith Model 49 in a clip holster under his shirt. It would be so easy to slip that hammerless snubnose baby out and pop Binny a nice .38 semijacket right in his sick skull...

And in the next moment, Rocco found that his right hand had moved to the revolver's slim grip.

"I called Vinchetti's crew and told them about the girl." Binny never took his eyes off the binocs. "Guaranteed them we'd have her in Jersey by morning. This time tomorrow night, we'll be partying hearty, paisan, with green in our pockets and neck-deep in snatch."

Rocco's fingers trailed off his piece. Vinchetti. Rocco knew he'd have to be very careful. Popping Binny right here would be suicide. He'd never beat Vinchetti's hawks without a plan. He needed papers, and cash. There was a printer he knew in Davidsonville who did good work; for a couple of grand he'd set Rocco up with a phony driver's license, SS number, birth cert, and an MVA record that would wash right up to a fed-level check. Good fake ID was the only way he'd get away from Vinchetti. There was only one option: *Just one more job. I'll do this one last job, take the cash, get my papers. Then I'll cap this evil fucker and disappear for good.* There was no other way. To buy good papers, he'd have to do this job on the old man and the girl first.

"Aw, God," Binny remarked. "Check it out."

Rocco took the glasses and focused up. The old man was sitting in the lit kitchen, at the table. "Big deal. He's eating dinner."

"No, no, man," Binny corrected. His breath was hot on Rocco's neck as he leaned over. "The bathroom. Tell me that ain't the sweetest stuff you ever saw. Vinchetti's gonna love us. That right there is pure angel food cake, partner."

You fuckin' slime, Rocco thought when he moved the binoculars. The kid stood buck naked, her blond hair tied up as she stepped out of the tub. She began to towel herself off under the bright light.

"Yeah, man." Binny grinned. "I could eat that myself."

Rocco reserved comment, electing instead to think, *I can't wait to take you down, Binny.* It provided a glorious fantasy. *Once I get my papers, I'm gonna put your fucked-up brains all over the floor.*

Binny chuckled. "Let's hit it."

They emerged from the trees, breaking off. Rocco's head pounded with each step. His last job, sure--but that didn't do the kid any good. She'd still be meat on Vinchetti's porno slab, and they'd have to kill the old man. *Just don't think about it,* he commanded himself. It was the lesser of two evils, that was the only way he could look at it. The back window popped open with just one press of the crowbar. Rocco climbed in.

A bedroom. Dark, but the door was open, and down the hall he could see the kitchen light, and the old man at the table.

Rocco set down the timer to free his hands; he moved into the hall. The kid was still in the bathroom-- the light glowed under the door. Binny already had a cord around the old man's neck by the time Rocco made it to the kitchen.

A pitiful sight. Binny grinned as the old man squirmed in the wheelchair, gagging. "Let him talk," Rocco complained.

"Just havin' a little fun first."

The old man's crabbed hands roved to and fro like a drunk conductor; his thin chest heaved. Just as the aged face began to turn blue, Binny loosened the garrotte.

"Blasted bastards!" the old man wheezed, hacking and bringing his arthritic fingers to his throat.

Binny grinned down. "Get to work, Roc. Me and Grandpa here have some talking to do."

"Get the hell out of my house, the both of you!" gargled Grandpa. "Ya got no right!"

"Sure we do, Gramps." Binny tightened the garrotte a bit. "We know you got cash stashed in this cozy little dump of yours." A little tighter. "So how about it, Gramps? Where's the money?"

Jaundiced eyes bulged in their sockets; the wizened mouth struggled. "Let him talk!" Rocco yelled. "You're killing him!"

"Relax." Again, Binny loosened the cord. The old man slumped, sucking breath and pointing to the floor. Eventually he was able to croak, "Baseboard. By the stove. Take it."

Binny knelt and pried out the board. "Christ, Roc! It's the fuckin' motherlode!" He slid out bands of bills, twenties and fifties. "There must be ten or fifteen grand here, man!"

"Closer to twenty," the old man coughed, waving a worm-veined hand. "Take it and get out of here. Leave us be."

"Oh, we will, Gramps." Binny chuckled and rose. "After we're done killing your tired ass. Huh, Roc?"

Rocco smirked, then suddenly jerked around. Feet pounded. A little blur swirled and at once small hands were dragging at him. The little girl jumped up onto Rocco's back and yanked his hair, shrieking: "Leave my grandpa alone!"

Binny laughed uproariously. Rocco turned in hunched circles, trying to keep the kid's fingers out of his eyes. When he flipped her to the floor, she sprang right back up and socked her little foot square into his groin. Rocco went down.

"Look at this!" Binny laughed. "One of Vinchetti's bulldogs is getting his ass whipped by a little kid!"

Rocco tried to wrestle the girl down, but she slipped out of his grasp like a greased lizard. *Shit!* Rocco thought. The girl banged through the door to the basement and scampered down.

Rocco got up, sputtering. At least there were no windows in the basement. No way the kid could go out.

"Go get her, killer," Binny mocked, then got back behind the old man, who futilely whipped his hands around. "Ya blasted punks!" he rasped. "Don't you hurt that little girl, I'm warnin' ya! Why, goddamn it all, if I wasn't in this blasted chair--"

"But you *are* in the chair, Gramps, you *are* in the chair," Binny ripped off that great old Bette Davis line.

Now the old man pleaded, his fine white hair sticking up as his face strained in the most desperate despair. "I'm beggin' ya not to do this. I got more money in the bank. I'll give it to ya, all of it. Just leave us alone..."

"This'll do us just fine, pops," Binny said. "See, we gotta deliver that sweet little girl of yours upstate tonight, so our friends can take some pretty pictures of her. And that means it's time for you to say goodnight."

The old man lurched, then hacked. Binny deftly brought the blade of his Gerber Mark IV straight across the throat.

Blood gushed, pumping. The old man hitched twice in the chair, gargled a final invective, then died.

Rocco felt enslimed. *Look at us,* he thought. *Two back-alley thugs fucking up little kids' lives and killing old men in wheelchairs. Christ almighty.*

"Don't just stand there, man," Binny complained, scooping up the banded cash off the floor. "Go get the girl. I'll get the joint ready to torch."

"Timer's in the back room," Rocco said. His heart felt sunken as he slid out the flask of Roche Pharmaceutical chloroform. "I'll bring her up now."

"Fuckin'-A. And be careful. That little hellfire's probably down there waiting for you with a pitchfork."

Or maybe a gun, Rocco mused. He almost wished it. He almost wished the kid would blow both their asses away.

"Get a move on!"

Rocco descended the creaky wood steps. Light wobbled from a suspended bulb. The little girl sat sobbing in the corner, her face long with despair and glazed by tears. Rocco poured some chloroform into his handkerchief.

What could he say? What could he tell this innocent little child? The chloroform wafted up, sickly sweet. "Come on, kid. You gotta come with us."

"You're the two men who've been following me," she sobbed.

"Yeah," Rocco said.

"But why?"

Why? The question haunted him. "I don't know why, kid. It's just the way things are sometimes."

The tears streamed. Strands of fine blond hair stuck to her face. "Grandpa said you wanted to do bad things to me. We haven't done bad things to you. Why do you want to do bad things to us?"

Rocco gulped. A simple question with no answer. He stared at her as her wet face peered up, her little feet tucked under her legs as she crouched in defeated terror and confusion. She wore a long flannel nightgown with rabbits on it. *Rabbits,* Rocco thought. *Bunny rabbits. She's just a little innocent kid, and I'm gonna deliver her to a bunch of child pornographers tonight. What kind of a monster am I?*

But he had no recourse, did he? The specter of Vinchetti's hatchetmen loomed behind him, a dark surging shape.

"I'm sorry, kid. I really am. But I got no choice."

Rocco moved forward, leaning down, and reached for the girl.

***

Binny rolled the dead old man out of the way, into the corner, then bagged the rest of the cash. *What a fuckin' haul!* Not only would they walk with decent scratch for the kid, but there was this in the baseboard. *Binny could use a beer,* he thought. *Yeah, a cold tall one. All this hard work makes a guy thirsty.* But when he opened the fridge all he found were some steaks and hamburger. Not a can of Bud to be found.

Rocco, he thought next, walking to the back bedroom. It was a sour thought. The guy was losing his edge, and this wasn't good. A job like this you don't bring your conscience. What was the big deal? It was like anything. When somebody wanted something, you got it for them, so long as the money was right. Supply and demand. That was the American Way, wasn't it?

He came back to the kitchen with the timer. Yeah, piece of fucking cake. "Hey, Roc!" he yelled. "Sometime this year, huh?" Christ. The gas range looked ancient. He figured they'd set the timer for a couple of hours, give the dump plenty of time to fill up. So what if he started a forest fire? That wasn't his problem. Smoky the Fucking Bear could worry about that.

What the fuck? he thought. He'd turned on the gas knobs, but no pilots came on, and no tell-tale hiss. He put his ear to the burner. Nothing. Then he slid the range out to take a peek.

The gas lines weren't even hooked up. *This thing hasn't been used in years,* he realized. And that didn't make a lick of sense, did it? A busted range and a fridge full of meat. He noticed no hotplates, no microwaves. What the hell did they cook their meat on?

This was a good question, not that it really mattered. What *did* matter, though, a moment later when he turned to the corner, was this:

The wheelchair was empty.

***

"Why?" the little girl sobbed just as Rocco stooped to press the handkerchief to her mouth. "Why? We haven't done anything bad to you!"

Rocco stared at the little thing. For a moment, he couldn't move. *What am I--* Then he dropped the chloroform-soaked rag.

The little girl was right.

"Fuck it," he said aloud. "I ain't doing it any more. The old man was already dead...but the kid? *It ain't gonna happen. What I do right now is I go back upstairs and I pop Binny. Then I take the cash and split, and Vinchetti never gets his paws on the girl. If she ID's me in a mugshot, then that's my tough luck.*

"Relax, kid," he said. "Your grandpa's dead, and I"m really sorry about that. But ain't nothing gonna happen to you. Things won't be that bad."

"It's-it's too late," the little girl said.

What did she mean by that? Rocco squinted at her. "Look, kid. I'm giving you a break here. I know it's hard but–"

--then his words were severed, cut off cleanly as a knife through yarn. Cut off by the wavering, high-pitched scream which exploded next from upstairs:

"HOLY JESUS CHRIST GET THE FUCK AWAY FROM ME!"

Rocco shucked his five-shot snub. His heart hammered as he raced up the stairs. Binny continued to scream, loud and hard–a sound more like a bad flywheel at high rev--when Rocco three-pointed into the kitchen. The first thing he saw made his eyes bulge.

The old man's wheelchair with no old man in it. No way the guy could've lived! Binny'd cut his throat clear to the bone.

And the second thing he saw...

Binny flailed frenetically on the floor beneath a dark form. It was not a dog which vigorously yanked out his partner's lower g.i. tract; it was a wolf. A big wolf.

Rocco emptied his bladder while he simultaneously emptied the Smith snub into the animal's side. Binny flinched, blood bubbling from his mouth. The huge animal paused only a moment at the shots, bit off Binny's face, then turned. Its great angular head rose, lips peeling back to show rows of crooked teeth the size of masonry nails. Jet black eyes bore into Rocco's stare. The eyes seemed mocking, even amused. Then the creature lunged.

Rocco missed having his throat bitten out by all of half an inch. He jerked back into the basement entrance, pulled the door closed, and fell head over heels to the bottom of the steps.

The little girl was standing now, her arms crossed over the rabbit-printed nightgown.

"See?" she said defiantly. "I told you."

Rocco's head spun. Upstairs he could hear the wolf return to its meal, bones crunching like potato chips. The image of the little girl bobbed back and forth like something floating.

"Your grandfather's a--"

"He's been that way for a long time," the girl said. "But he's always been good. You should've been good, too."

Rocco stared at her. Upstairs, the crunching went on and on.

"Nobody has to be bad. It's better to be good," the little girl philosophized. "I'm the same way. Just little animals and things." She pointed to the corner of the basement, to little piles of animals that looked dried as husks.

"Never people," she said. Then her face seemed to flutter, as if adrift in an intricate confusion. "Well, almost never."

Rocco felt paralyzed. He couldn't get up. He couldn't even look away from the big, glittering eyes.

"You're just like your grandfather," Rocco croaked.

"No I'm not," the little girl said.

Did she smile?

"I'm a lot worse."

She moved forward very slowly. Her twin incisors glinted like nails.

The End

Other Books by KJK Publishing

Collections
Dark Thoughts
Vampiro and Other Strange Tales of the Macabre
Merry Fuckin' Christmas and Other Yuletide Shit!
The A to Z of Horror

Anthologies
Collected Christmas Horror Shorts
Collected Easter Horror Shorts
Collected Halloween Horror Shorts
Collected Christmas Horror Shorts 2
Collected Christmas Horror Shorts 3
The Horror Collection: Gold Edition
The Horror Collection: Black Edition
The Horror Collection: Purple Edition
The Horror Collection: White Edition
The Horror Collection: Silver Edition
The Horror Collection: Pink Edition
The Horror Collection: Emerald Edition
The Horror Collection: Pumpkin Edition
The Horror Collection: Yellow Edition
The Horror Collection: Ruby Edition
The Horror Collection: Extreme Edition
The Horror Collection: Nightmare Edition
The Horror Collection: Sapphire Edition
The Horror Collection: The Lost Edition
The Horror Collection: LGBTQIA+ Edition
The Horror Collection: Monster Edition
The Horror Collection: Sci-Fi Edition
The Horror Collection: Turquoise Edition

100 Word Horrors
100 Word Horrors 2
100 Word Horrors 3
100 Word Horrors 4
Carnival of Horror
Inside the Indie Horror World (Non fiction)
Vampires

Novels and Novellas
Pandemonium by J.C. Michael
You Only Get One Shot by Kevin J. Kennedy & J.C. Michael
Screechers by Kevin J. Kennedy & Christina Bergling
Stitches by Steven Stacy & Kevin J. Kennedy
Halloween Land by Kevin J. Kennedy

Printed in Great Britain
by Amazon